THE RETURNING TIDE

THE RETURNING TIDE

JULIA SOKOTA

Matador
9 Priory Business Park,
Wistow Road, Kibworth Beauchamp,
Leicestershire. LE8 0RX
Tel: (+44) 116 279 2299
Fax: (+44) 116 279 2277
Email: books@troubador.co.uk
Web: www.troubador.co.uk/matador

ISBN 978-1783065-523

British Library Cataloguing in Publication Data.
A catalogue record for this book is available from the British Library.

Typeset in 12pt Bembo by Troubador Publishing Ltd, Leicester, UK
Printed and bound in the UK by TJ International, Padstow, Cornwall

Matador is an imprint of Troubador Publishing Ltd

For Siân and Vanessa

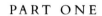
PART ONE

1

Last night I dreamt of the sea, a beach, and a child.

It is over now. I knew that yesterday when I left that cursed land full of promise and desolation and, once more, vowed never to set foot in Cornwall again.

It is time to write my story. I need to leave the record straight for those I have wronged and may never see again. I will not escape censure and judgement will be harsh, but forced disclosure in public would be more than I could endure.

We all build our lives on some form of deception known only to ourselves; it is how we survive and our secrets are rarely exposed. Even now I still dare to hope, for it is hope that sustained me all those years ago and gave me the will to carry on. Although recent events compel me to face reality and oblige me to write, my story may never be read. My reputation, so assiduously preserved, may yet remain.

It depends on the phone call I know she will make later this morning.

2

I first went to Cornwall when I was ten years old and the memory of that holiday, luminous and magical, stayed with me for years. I went with my father and mother to the far South West, 'to the end of the line,' as my father said.

The guest-house was owned by a Mrs. Carter who is probably dead by now. I remember her because she always spoke to me, paid me more attention. While my parents ate their full English breakfast, she, observing that I had struggled with the salty bacon, the slippery fried eggs and the slimy mushrooms, prepared two boiled eggs, slightly hard, with buttered brown bread soldiers. I did not like toast because once, some months earlier, the sharp bits had stuck in my throat and I had nearly choked to death, although my parents had said that was an exaggeration, as was my response at that age to certain foods. On our second morning there, Mrs. Carter set down a rack of toast for my parents and then brought in a special plate for me, saying, 'There you are, my handsome, a nice soft scone with a bit of jam and Cornish cream. That will slide down.'

My parents liked walking, so we walked across rugged cliffs and moors in a remote, untamed landscape, the very stuff of legend. It was a hot summer that year and most of all I remember lazy afternoons on beaches, cool, clear water and the steep climb to the top of St. Michael's Mount, where I gazed in wonder at that wide expanse of ocean across Mount's Bay, the small sailing boats and the green and gentle coast line.

I loved the sea in those days. I loved the tepid warmth as it slapped over my feet and ankles, cooling as it reached my knees. By the time it reached my body it was colder, and I shivered. 'Dip down! Down, quickly, over your shoulders, it's better that way,' said my father. Shockingly cold, it took my breath away for mere seconds before suffusing my whole body in smooth and soothing coolness. I learnt to swim that summer.

These were my childhood memories of Cornwall, memories reinforced over the years by Polaroid snapshots. I longed to go back, the three of us together, but we never did. Summers were usually spent in France. My father's mother was French and we stayed with her and my uncle and aunt. Their vineyard produced good wine most of which was sold locally although some was exported to Holland, Belgium and England, thanks mainly to my grandfather who had looked after that side of the business; when he died, my father, who owned one of the two off-licences in our small Sussex town, took it over. It was then that my grandmother returned to France – 'to my wonderful chateau' – and, after that, each year, our holidays were spent, dutifully, in France.

Had it not been for that matchless holiday I would never have harboured memories which grew, as the years passed, into expectations with which time could never realistically compete. Situations change and we change with them, the feelings we attach to memories can rarely be repeated and some are best forgotten.

★

So it was, some thirteen years later, my father having been dead for six of them, I went once more to Cornwall. I could have gone straight to France instead, I had reason enough to do so, but I wanted to revisit places I only partially remembered and recall a time of artless childhood pleasure. I also thought I could establish a closer relationship with my child, then two years old, if there were just the two of us, together for once.

We stayed in a small, two bedroomed terraced house, one of nine identical houses, each with a small front garden facing the main road. There was a good-sized back garden, with herbaceous borders and a large tree near the back gate. Just a few yards away, by the side of the house, a lane, quite wide and busy, led down to the beach. Further along the main road, there was a small row of shops, a general store, a greengrocer, a bakery and a fish and chip shop.

Four of the houses in Pensquidden Terrace were owned by the same family. Mr. Evans lived in one and let the others to tourists during the summer. Mr. and Mrs. Goodman, a friendly, middle-aged couple from Liverpool, were staying next door to us and on the day we arrived they invited us to join them for tea in the garden. It was the Goodmans who, three days after we arrived, took us out to lunch at the Tregeagle Inn, some six or seven miles from where we lived, because it had a play area for children.

As you approach the Tregeagle Inn from the road, you see a squat, forbidding castle with little turrets sticking up above the heavy dark walls with small windows, the frames painted black. It was a nineteenth century folly, designed to appeal to the darker side of myth and legend.

Having made a pact with the Devil, the Tregeagle is

doomed, like Sisyphus, to work on impossible tasks which can never be completed, or he will fall into hell for all eternity. His wild spirit, with ghostly wailing, roams across the valleys and moors of Cornwall, through the depths of tin mines and across tempestuous seas, instilling fear in all who hear him.

Inside, presumably as an atmospheric tribute to the Tregeagle, the main bar was dark and gloomy; walls and low wooden beams were covered with pictures of shipwrecks, huge waves towering over piers and promenades, wild windswept moors and tin miners digging in the deep bowels of the earth.

From the road, you cannot see the back of the inn. Here, a large extension, all white plaster and glass, had been built in recent years, so completely different in style from the original building that you wonder how planning permission was ever given. This was a modern restaurant, bright and airy, with huge windows facing the lawned grounds, which had more tables and chairs for those who wished to eat outside, and there was a play area beyond with swings, a slide and a sandpit for children. It was thoughtfully designed, a pleasant, relaxing place with a reputation for good food.

It was a bizarre, irrational building, but in those days I liked it; its very incongruity appealed to the romantic side of my nature and it was here that I met Mark.

'We're here again,' Mrs. Goodman said as the waiter handed us the menu. 'We've brought our friends this time,' and she glanced in our direction, 'we thought they'd find this place rather unusual.'

'Nothing is quite as it seems here, it's like walking from heaven to hell in thirty steps,' Mark said and those were the first words I heard him say, the first time he looked at me and smiled.

Mark: pub waiter, barman, child-friendly mopper of tables, seasonal employee; otherwise chemistry postgraduate at Bristol, his Ph.D. thesis near completion; well-mannered, helpful, modest and slightly shy, a winning quality in someone young, energetic, tall and good looking. The attraction was instant and we fell in love soon after, madly, ecstatically, blissfully in love. I loved him more than any man I've ever loved, before or since.

He followed us out when we were leaving to say there would be a clown to entertain the children the following afternoon, 'if your little girl would be interested, two o'clock in the play area.' I saw the relief and the delighted smile when I said, 'Yes, I think she would be.' On the way back, Mrs. Goodman said, 'I think you've made a conquest, dear.'

The following day we had gone to see the clown and Mark invited us to a Disney film on his half day off, he thought Krystina would like it. After that we spent what time we could to be together, which was little more than two half days a week as he worked long hours during the busiest months of the season. One evening, as the Goodmans had offered to babysit, we went to a disco in Falmouth together and, twice a week, we had tea together with his parents at their house, not far from the Tregeagle Inn. I often took Krystina to the inn for lunch; the food was good, the play area useful, and although, in those two or three hours, Mark would be busy serving food and drinks, we were always able to snatch some time together.

Krystina was happy. 'See Mark today?' she would ask each morning. 'Go to Trickle?'

'It's Tregeagle, Krystina. Say, Treg …ea …gle.'

' …Trig … Trickle.'

Trickle it remained and, amused by her attempts to pronounce the word, Mark always used her name for the inn when the three of us were together.

Three weeks of unexpected, unimagined happiness! Three weeks that would end with Mark running across a beach, breathless, words tumbling from his mouth, 'Marry me! Let's get married!'

'What took you so long to ask?' I said laughing, as he threw his arms around me, then took off his shirt, for I was wet from the sea, and put it around my shoulders. 'And why are you so late? You said you'd be here at two and now it's five o'clock. I was getting worried!' 'Road accident. Thought I'd never get here. I kept thinking, what if she's gone? What if I never see her again?' I laughed, 'I would have come to the Tregeagle tomorrow, of course.'

We scrambled up a couple of rocks, sat down on a lower white one. He told me about the collision between a car and an articulated lorry which had blocked the road for nearly three hours, how he just had to wait, becoming more anxious, almost desperate, as he realized, was absolutely certain, that there was no one else in the world for him but me. And so, lying there on that secluded rock, we fell into each other's arms with passionate expressions of love, happily oblivious to the world and everyone in it but ourselves.

But I digress. I did not know then that my life was about to change forever. It is enough to say that I went to Cornwall that year, now thirty years ago, with good intentions, motivated by a childhood memory and I left with other memories that would craze my dreams, even in lighted bedrooms far from home, for years.

Memories haunted me down the years, a persistent nagging presence like a dormant volcano, which could erupt dangerously at any moment, threatening my existence and the lives of those I loved. Those years of exile, wandering across the world in a constant state of trepidation, were the worst.

Yet, slowly, as the past receded, it took the fear and dreams with it and hope, love, gratitude, all rose unexpectedly and confidently, like a new dawn. I had refashioned my life and I returned to a promising and successful future. The need for vigilance was always there, but it no longer preoccupied me for every minute of the day. There were weeks and months in the years that followed when I was at ease with myself, gratefully happy and secure within a loving family and untroubled by past events. It helped that my two homes are in Sussex and France and a long way from Cornwall.

★

And now, this year, thirty years later, I went again to Cornwall. I did not want to go, I never wanted to set foot in that part of the country again. It was definitely not my choice and against my better judgement.

Cornwall has become fashionable among young people with money to spare; some have even bought cottages, homes for long weekends or for a few weeks a year which they may let out to friends. Krystina went to Cornwall with a friend last year, just for three days, near Boscastle, and claimed she fell in love with the place. I wasn't happy about it, but it was in the far north of Cornwall and only for a short time.

This year she decided to stay for a month, part holiday, part work, in a cottage with two bedrooms near St. Ives. She wanted me to join her but I made excuses. She tried again when she arrived there.

'Mum, it's so lovely here! You can go for walks along the coast, visit little villages, old churches full of saints you've never heard of, there's so much to see and do. Of course, you know all that. Grandma told me how much you loved Cornwall when you were a child. James and Anna are here as well for the first week. Please come and stay! You haven't had a holiday since Dad died. A month in Cornwall will do you good!'

I still refused, but three days into their holiday James also began pestering me to join them. 'You are being unreasonable and obstinate,' he said, admonishing me, before adding, 'Come on, Mum, you'll enjoy it. Krys won't want to be here all on her own for three weeks. Make us happy.'

I could think of no satisfactory excuse to refuse, in some ways it would have been unreasonable, even selfish, to do so. It also occurred to me that it might be better if I were there. I may have some control over what we did, where we went. Common sense told me it could do no harm, that I was letting my imagination run away with me.

That is how, with many misgivings, I agreed to go to Cornwall. I could not foresee what would happen: an ill-timed discovery, a latent memory rising from the subconscious mind, then a chance encounter, nothing more than a coincidence. With what frightening rapidity has the

11

past been brought into the present! And it is Krystina, who loves me as I love her, who has, unwittingly, done this. It is Krtystina, like Nemesis herself, who threatens me now.

3

We have a good mother-daughter relationship; everyone remarks on how well we get on. We do love each other, although, in the beginning, it was not that instinctive love which we are supposed to feel at first sight and which, indeed, I felt when James was first placed in my arms. Rather, Krystina and I grew to love each other and it took time and trust to deepen the bond between us. Such differences in maternal love are not that unusual, many a mother must have experienced this.

Children need love and a stable home life. James had this from me from the beginning, Krystina, a little later. It is something that has concerned me over the years, but both children have turned out well, they are kind, decent people, they are successful in their work. I am proud of them.

After studying in England and France, James became a vintner and he has taken over much of the work of the family business. He has been married to Anna, an accountant, for nearly a year and they say they want to have children as soon as they are more settled, which probably depends on whether they will make their main home in France or England. James thinks ahead, his risks are well calculated, and he trusts his own judgement in his dealings with people. He takes after Jeff, maybe even my father, in that respect.

At one time, I had hoped that Krystina would take over the family business, but she has chosen a different path; perhaps, on reflection, not so surprising for she is a thinker, well suited to academic life with its long hours of analytical research. After her first class law degree at a good red-brick university, she concentrated on social policy and ethics for her doctorate, which was later published. Since then, she has published several articles and has just finished one about the effect of social legislation on meeting the needs of vulnerable children, particularly those in care or facing adoption. She is a senior lecturer at a London university and two of her colleagues have told me that she is likely to be a professor within a year.

She is often asked to give talks at conferences for professionals involved in child protection; and she has the ability to present and argue a case with persuasive conviction. She has already served on two influential working parties, which have played a part in shaping government policy. If you are in that line of work, you may have heard of Krystina Bentley.

After the first somewhat distressing five years of her life, I must take some credit for the way I brought her up and the opportunities I gave her. Even my mother, and God knows how critical she was, said, only a few years ago and not long before first, dementia, then death, took her away from us, 'You've done well with that girl of yours; and James as well, although you had Jeff there from the beginning. But you did well with Krystina in spite of everything. I'll give you your due, Claire.'

Krystina has never come close to getting married. Her relationships – and there have been three or four that I know of – last, at most, for a few months. Just as you hope something may come of one, she is uncertain, doesn't know, feels it won't last. There's an element of insecurity. She tends to be cautious and selective in her choice of friends, and although she knows many people and is on amicable terms with them, only two or three are close friends. She is totally committed to her work, committed to finding answers to social problems and ethical issues, and it is this that gives most meaning to her life.

In some ways she's like Jeff. His influence, his unstinting encouragement over the years, must have rubbed off. Flesh and blood isn't everything, whatever they say. An adoptive parent can be as good, even better than one who merely supplied the genes. Krystina knows this, she doesn't need to say so. Once, when she was at school, she had to do a family tree for homework. She was happy to get enough ancestral details from me and from Jeff and count them both as her own; and once she had done her homework she had no further interest in distant ancestors.

I really cannot understand the present fascination with tracing unknown relations. It has become a fashionable hobby now; quite a business with *Who were your ancestors? Nineteenth century census now on line* and television programmes delving into the past of the famous. Some, who have little better to do, spend hours tracing people they do not know and can never know, but whose genes they think they have inherited, however diluted, and for what? What do they gain from it? Some names, dates and possible employment which may have changed from one year to the next, and sometimes cause of death which may not even be accurate. It is very unreliable, anyway. One slip, one conception out of the marital bed – and there must have been many – and the whole tree grows in the wrong direction, in need of drastic pruning, which nobody recognizes. I have no time for it. It is what you are and what you do that counts, not where you come from and a family tree of all your relatives. Nature may play a part, but it is very small compared with nurture, especially when the nurture gives children the love and stability that they need, as well as opportunity and even privilege.

Krystina was devoted to Jeff and she has shown much concern and affection for me since I became a widow. She is not over demonstrative and when, on the odd occasion, I see her gazing into space, she always says she is thinking about work and I think she is. But these times are much fewer now than when she was a child. Then she would sit staring ahead for a long time, until I managed to distract her with some activity, a trip to the beach, to a local park, to places where we could see wild animals, or, later, a visit to friends.

I married Jeff in New Zealand when Krystina was five. I sat down with both of them and told her, 'Your daddy went away soon after you were born. He saw you two or three times when you were a little baby and then he had to go away and he never came back. Jeff is now your daddy and he isn't ever going away. He is going to stay with you and mummy forever. Soon, you will have a new name and so will I. So all three of us will have the same name.'

'Another name?' she said, her eyes wide with confusion or, perhaps, distress.

'Yes,' I said quickly. 'We won't be called Moreton any more, we'll be called Bentley, the same as Jeff. You'll like that won't you? Of course, you'll still be called Krystina, that's the most important name.'

She seemed to accept this in her quiet way and soon began to cling to Jeff as much as she clung to me. When, the following year, James was born I told her we had given her a brother, all for herself. We were a complete family of four, living in New Zealand and making arrangements to return to England.

I remember her raising the issue only once, when she was in her teens. They had been discussing teenage pregnancies in her class that day.

'You weren't a teenage mother, were you?' she said.

It was a rhetorical question and I recognized it for what it was, a question to lead somewhere else.

'No, I said, 'I was twenty, nearly twenty one and old enough to know better.'

'You know, I'm not sure if I remember his name, you have told me, ages ago, but I've forgotten.'

'Ricky,' I said, light and cheerful. 'Ricky Tyler. At least, that's what he was known by. He was the lead guitarist in *The Ravers*, a promising northern group. They became better known when *Love me, love me,* and *Losing you* got into the charts. They had a six-month stint in the south hoping to make their name and fortune and follow in the footsteps of *The Beatles*, or *The Rolling Stones*, or any other group which made a million or two and became a household name. His real name was Richard Taylor and the group, like so many others, after some initial success, disbanded after a couple of years and disappeared from the scene.'

She was quiet for a while. 'I suppose it was during the six month stint?'

'Yes, that's very astute of you!'

'What was he like? Did you like him?'

I laughed. 'Of course I liked him! He was good-looking, fun to be with and very popular. I'll show you a photo. You will have seen it before, but perhaps you've forgotten.'

I fetched the photo of both of us together and another of the band. She studied them thoughtfully. 'Did you really wear clothes like that?'

'It was the fashion. We thought we looked wonderful, of course. But then, we were young and we were in love, or thought we were.'

'But he left you. And me.'

'Don't think too badly of him. Ricky meant well and in his way did care about us or tried to. But he was young, ambitious, too captivated by the promise of pop-star success to take on other responsibilities. He may have left, but I didn't want him to stay.'

'You didn't? Not when … '

'No, it would have been a dreadful mistake. I met him at a rather lonely time in my life and he seemed to be the best thing that had happened to me since my father died. Grandma did her best, of course, but her time was taken up with running the shop on her own and in the evenings she was tired and still missing my father. And I wasn't exactly a bundle of joy to live with.'

'Would it have been such a mistake?'

'It would have been wrong for both of us and it wouldn't have lasted. He was only really interested in his music and I confused infatuation with love.'

'I remember you said once that he did see me.'

'Oh, yes, He came down from Manchester, where the band was then playing, soon after you were born and he came again a few weeks later. We kept in touch for a while. He sent birthday and Christmas cards with some money for the first two or three years, but we gradually lost touch after we went to Australia and then Jeff took over.'

'What happened to him?'

'He went back up north, somewhere near Manchester. He got involved with the music trade, recordings, hi-fi equipment, that sort of thing. I know he was thinking of opening a business abroad at that stage, possibly South Africa. For all I know, he might have emigrated there.'

'South Africa? During apartheid?'

I knew that would condemn him in her eyes. 'Well, so I heard, I don't know for sure. When we wrote asking if Jeff could adopt you, we received the reply from his solicitor and all dealings were done through him. And that is the last we heard from him.' I hesitated a moment before venturing to say, 'You can keep the photos. If you want you could try to track him down some time.'

'No, I already have a father. There's no need.' She gave me back the photos.

This is the story I told Krystina and Jeff. It was consistent. It never faltered. Krystina had a good father in Jeff, she adored him and never asked another question about Ricky Tyler. Jeff, when I told him about Krystina's birth, soon after meeting him, looked at me with great tenderness and said: 'I admire you, I really do. Ricky Tyler was a fool to lose you, but I'm glad he did.'

Dear, kind, loving Jeff! I miss him. He never knew how grateful I was.

★

My story was not entirely true. Ricky Tyler, lead guitarist of *The Ravers* did exist and although I was not so besotted with him, there was some kudos in being the girlfriend of one of *The Ravers*. I did like him, was attracted to him, maybe even more than I was to Pierre in France.

The truth is, I was already three months pregnant when I realized it, otherwise I would have done something about it. The pregnancy, unwanted at first, and Ricky's nervous, lukewarm attitude to it, forced me to evaluate our relationship and I found it wanting. We liked each other, the physical attraction was mutual, but it was sustained through what seemed, at the time, to be an exciting lifestyle, part of the magnetic allure of pop culture. Our relationship was superficial, there was not enough depth or substance in it for marriage. I turned down Ricky's rambling, almost incoherent offer of marriage and said I wanted a symphony, not a pop tune, and a compromise wouldn't be fair to either of us. He accepted my refusal with kindhearted expressions of regret, delivered with a certain degree of alacrity.

★

A year later, when I was in hospital, the psychiatrist who spent the odd half hour with me, claimed that I was in search of affection and attributed my breakdown to the death of my father, which, she claimed, had emotionally destabilized me.

My father died suddenly when I was seventeen. I had been alone with him in the shop that evening when he suddenly clutched his chest, lurched against the counter, stayed there for seconds while I stood watching, my brain trying to process what had happened, and then he fell to the floor. I rushed to him and knelt beside him. His eyes were closed, his mouth partly open, his skin grey. I loosened his tie, undid his top shirt button, went to the phone and dialed 999. The call seemed to take forever, while I gave name, address, and a description of what had happened. 'Please hurry!' I shouted, 'Come at once!' I was told the ambulance would be there within ten minutes and to give him an aspirin. When I went back he was no longer breathing and my ear, close to his heart, detected no sound at all.

I felt a strong sense of guilt that I was unable to help him, that I had not somehow noticed that he was ill. It was my first experience of death, the first traumatic event of my young life.

My mother immersed herself in work, put on a brave face and carried on. I resented her for it, quite unfairly, for they were close, my parents; I know now that her quiet, stoical acceptance of his death hid a grief at least equal to mine.

I could talk to no one about it and I felt strangely isolated at the time. I felt a loneliness in grief which was only alleviated by sleep, that debilitating tiredness which keeps you in bed all morning, unable to face the reality of an empty world, until that instinct the young have for self preservation turned morning lassitude into evenings of hyperactivity. Then I needed company, the offer of instant friendships, shared drug-fuelled trips, wild, neon-lit discos where noise drowned out unwanted thoughts.

I failed my A levels – well, three of them, although I got a B for French. This, after five As and three Bs at GCSE was a disappointment not just for my teachers, but for my mother. Newly widowed, she mourned my father and moaned at me: 'You had such an opportunity, the world was your oyster. But you had to go out drinking and dancing, mixing with the wrong type and sleeping it off until two in the afternoon. You wouldn't have done it if your father were alive. Now what will you do?'

She wanted me to go back to school, to retake my A levels, but I could not face another year at school. So I worked in the shop helping my mother and the two part-time assistants who had been with us for years. I spent the following summer in France with my grandmother, working in the vineyard at grape picking time. Grapes were interesting. I liked the whole process of changing them into wine. I was much better there. I led a more normal life. I had a fling with one of the seasonal workers – Pierre – but we were discrete, my grandmother never knew, or, if she did, for there was not much that passed her notice, she never mentioned it.

But when I returned, a heavy weight of emptiness descended upon me. I felt I should be doing something with my life, but I didn't know what. School and university no longer interested me. Home stifled me and I fell back into my old ways. I would get to the shop in the late afternoon, work manically while I was there, serving customers, checking stock, ordering supplies, and leave after nine, go home, change, and head for the discos and clubs, returning home at four in the morning.

It was at this time that *The Ravers* were playing at *The Starlight Express,* a new upmarket club in town and it was there that I met Ricky Tyler. Soon I was staying out overnight, two or three times a week at Ricky's place, a run-down flat the group had rented for three months. I was not entirely irresponsible for I was on the pill, but one gets careless when preoccupied, or befuddled with drink, or the occasional recreational drug.

'Now, see what you've done!' my mother said when I told her, 'Got yourself in trouble and trouble which will last you for years, maybe a lifetime. Is this boy – Ricky someone, a steady boyfriend? Is he going to help you out?'

As I made no answer to these questions, she continued, 'You've ruined your chances of settling down with some nice, decent man who would look after you. What are you going to do now?'

I was going to have the baby. I had no choice. Anyway, it would be someone to look after, to care for, to give meaning to my life. In some ways, it came as a relief. I would have to remove myself from the social scene, retreat peacefully into myself, something I had been incapable of doing. It was something to live for.

I was surprised that I felt this way. I could not explain why I did. The pregnancy did not bother me and I certainly didn't care what people thought. I did a four-day First Aid course with St. John's Ambulance, I read books about babies, bought baby clothes. I would be a good mother. I was happier than I had been for the past three years. Yet looking back, there was something too brashly confident, too extreme about it, too unreal.

'I don't know what you're so happy about,' my mother said when I was six months pregnant. 'There'll be tough times ahead, it's not a piece of cake, you know.'

I took no notice. Her opinions did not matter. Drink, drugs, parties, men, no longer interested me. The baby was all that mattered. I blossomed like a hothouse flower.

The actual birth was another matter. A prolonged labour, indifferent staff, being left alone for hours while the husbands of other mothers stayed by their bedsides, holding hands, checking times of contractions, just being there, being involved. The delivery was difficult and unbearably painful. They took the baby away. 'Just checking,' they said, and told me no more.

My mother arrived, soon after she was born. 'Well, I told you it wouldn't be a piece of cake,' she said when she saw me looking tired and uncomfortable, but her voice was not unsympathetic. 'She's a lovely little thing. They've been monitoring her breathing but she's fine. Have you seen her yet?'

They brought her in to me soon after, but it was just a baby, cleaned and wrapped up. I felt nothing, only a great tiredness and discomfort when I moved. I wanted to escape from this hospital bed and this pink, crinkled, meaningless face and from my mother who was beaming full of pride, as if she had given birth to it herself.

'I want to sleep now,' I said.

I did everything one should. I fed and changed it, bathed it, dried it, picked it up when it cried, took it out in the pram.

My mother helped and it was she who gushed over the baby, talking to it, singing it to sleep. I was grateful because I knew I could not have coped on my own; so, after two weeks, when I still had not chosen a name, I said I would like to call her after my mother. My mother thought a baby should have its own individual name, so as my mother's name was Christine, I chose Krystina, with a K. 'Similar but different, that's nice,' said my mother and I think she was pleased.

Ricky came down from Manchester, where they had been performing, soon after Krystina was born. He looked at the tiny, crumpled little thing in the cot and tried hard to be interested. He stared at her, not sure what to say. 'She's very nice,' he said eventually and after a few minutes he said it again. He gave me £50, the equivalent of his takings for a week and said he would come and see her again and he would send money. He called again about six weeks later. 'Oh, she's grown,' he said, 'she's much bigger now.'

He did not call again, although we kept in contact and he always sent a card with a very generous gift of money at Christmas. It all stopped when I went to Australia. I heard from him only once more. He wrote at the same time that I heard from his solicitor agreeing to the adoption. Ricky may have been selfish and immature, like so many other young people, but he was not entirely irresponsible and he had a conscience.

He said he regretted that it had come to this, but recognized that it was in Krystina's interest to be part of a proper family with a father who, by all accounts, was dependable and fond of her. He said he had no wish to interfere in our new life but, if, in time, Krystina wanted to make contact with him, he would be pleased and he could always be contacted either at the above address or through the solicitor, who would always be informed of his whereabouts. He said he was sorry he had made such a mess of things and he would never forget us.

I told no one about the letter. I tore it up into tiny bits and threw them in the fire.

4

I assumed my feelings for the baby would change, that I would eventually bond with her, but the days lengthened into weeks and looking after her was tiring work. She was a testy, demanding baby who rarely slept for more than two hours at a time, who seemed to be constantly hungry but refused to be fed for more than a few minutes; she was unhappy lying down and only mildly content if you were walking up and down with her all the time. When my mother returned from the shop, she always found me, at the end of the day, exhausted. The baby drained every bit of energy out of me. Sometimes, when she started crying, I burst into tears myself.

One day, when Krystina was three months old, my mother came home from the shop in the middle of the afternoon and found me still in bed. Krystina had not been fed, changed or washed. She was crying weakly where I had put her early that morning, downstairs in a carrycot, hungry and soaking wet.

I refused to get up. My mother left the room and a few minutes later Krystina stopped crying. It may have been half an hour later that my mother, with the doctor, walked into my bedroom. I was furious with her for calling him and when he spoke and started asking me questions I said I didn't want to speak to anyone.

'Go away,' I said, 'I'm too tired to talk. You have no right to be here. I didn't send for you.'

He adopted a soothing tone, trying to coax me out from under the bedclothes, as if I were little more than a baby myself.

'I told you to go! Didn't you hear me? Now, get out of my room!' I shouted.

'Oh, I'm so sorry, doctor,' I heard my mother murmur, clearly discomfited by my outburst.

'It's all right, Mrs. Moreton,' his voice as smooth as oil, and I couldn't catch the rest, but I heard the words 'depression' and 'rejection', before the phrase 'it happens sometimes, under these circumstances.'

A wild fury inflamed me and I sat abruptly up in bed; the very room seemed hazardous, the two figures near the door, hostile and threatening. I grabbed the nearest thing on the bedside table, which happened to be a small clock set in green serpentine, which my father had bought at the Lizard during that holiday eleven years ago. This I threw at the pair as they were leaving the room, shouting, 'Get out! Get out! Leave me alone! You, and the fucking baby!'

The clock hit the doctor on the back of his head. He stumbled, lurched forward and almost fell. I just saw a splash of blood on his white collar before I sank down in the bed, pulling the duvet up over my head, my heart pounding wildly.

They left me alone and the house was eerily quiet for several minutes. Then the bedroom door opened and my mother and two paramedics came in.

They spoke gently: 'Now, get out of bed, love. You can get on the stretcher or you can walk out with us and we'll take you to hospital. You'll feel better there, they'll look after you.'

I said nothing, but I got out of bed. My legs felt full of jelly and I struggled to put one foot in front of the other. They put a blanket around my shoulders and each supported me on either side as I walked down the stairs, like a very frail, old woman, to the ambulance outside. My mother came with me, so did the doctor, pressing on a large surgical dressing which the paramedic had put on his head.

At the hospital I was put in the psychiatric unit. I just about remember a doctor, some nurses, an injection and nothing after that for what may have been several hours or several days.

'Nice to see you again,' I said, somewhat offhandedly, when my mother arrived.

She looked surprised. 'I've been here each day, sometimes twice, since you were admitted last Tuesday. You've been sleeping and waking, sleeping and waking. You never spoke.'

'Oh,' I said, thinking hard. 'I don't remember.'

'You've had a nervous breakdown. The doctor had to call the ambulance. I wouldn't have agreed, but I had no choice after you threw the clock at him. He needed three stitches.'

'Oh,' I said, not really sure what response I should make to this.

'So, now that you are more awake, how is everything here? It all seems very nice.'

I told her I had done a word association test that morning, then I had talked to someone called Judith who wanted to know about significant people in my life and things I often thought about.

29

'Judith is the psychiatrist. I've met her, she's very nice. They're all trying to help you, Claire.'

'How long will I be here?'

'It depends on the progress you make. It may be a month or two, it all depends. They won't let you out until they're sure.'

'Sure of what?'

'Sure that you're well enough, that you can cope with everything, sure that you are yourself.'

'But I am myself. Whose self would I be?'

'They want you to be in control of yourself, Claire, not out of control – not that you could help it, of course – but it was a violent attack and he needed three stitches. And Krystina had not been fed for hours, she was hungry and wet. So you will be properly assessed and only let out when they are sure you are back to normal, – well, of course, you're normal, a lot of people get nervous breakdowns, – what I meant was, back to your old self, because you haven't been yourself, I mean, like you used to be, for ages, have you?'

I wondered which self she was thinking of. I knew I had changed and for a moment I saw myself through her eyes. It couldn't have been easy for her.

I had been diagnosed with post-traumatic stress and post-natal depression. Many women suffer from post-natal depression and some end up on antidepressants and this is all that would have happened to me if only I had not thrown the clock, or if I had thrown it on the floor, or if it had just hit the door instead of the doctor. Blood and stitches were evidence of a violent, unprovoked attack, so I was considered dangerous, dangerous to myself and others, including the baby. They kept me in hospital for two months and in a relatively short time I fully recovered. It was an episode in my life scarcely worth mentioning although, at times, it has been useful for me to do so.

During those months in hospital my mother had employed Diane, a young cousin of one of the shop assistants, to help in the shop in the morning while she stayed at home with Krystina. Later, she would go to the shop and Diane would come to the house to do any work that needed doing and look after the baby. When I came out of hospital my mother continued this arrangement, she said it would make things easier for me and it did. I recognized that I was under supervision and that this was as much for the baby's benefit as it was for mine.

Diane was nineteen and was attending evening classes twice a week in hospitality studies at the local college. She came from a large family and was glad of the extra work. We got on well. She was a decent, level-headed girl and we became good friends.

Krystina had grown, she was more settled, and now that I was not alone with her for hours she was easier to manage. A few months later the doctor reduced my medication to the minimum dosage, saying I was doing well and would soon be off it altogether. I apologized for the three stitches and he shrugged and waved his hands dismissively, as if to say it didn't matter at all.

At the end of six months I was well enough to go back to work and decided to find a proper job with a proper salary. I felt better and was, as my mother said, more myself. My mother spent more time at the shop, while Diane took care of Krystina and I started work as a receptionist for Nichols and Wilson, the biggest firm of solicitors in town.

There I thrived and after six months they increased my salary, saying I was reliable and competent, a good communicator with a knack for putting clients at ease. Nothing boosts your confidence or increases your sense of self-worth as much as praise. I felt that I had been lost in some dense, impenetrable quagmire and had emerged finally into bright, clean sunshine.

I had given up the discos, the drugs and the drink. I drank a little wine sometimes, always the family wine and only with meals. I met up with friends, but most nights I stayed in, reading or watching television and sometimes playing with Krystina. I didn't mind living at home. Diane was very good with Krystina, my mother adored her, I liked the job and the arrangement suited us.

In time I may have wanted more challenging work and a place of my own. My life may have lacked a certain purpose and excitement, but for those two years following my stay in the hospital, I was at peace with myself and content enough.

★

The change in my life came suddenly and unexpectedly. My grandmother in France had a stroke and after a few days of telephone calls it became clear that she was critically ill. My mother and I flew to Paris and took a train to Tours and then on to the chateaux a few miles north of Chenin, close to the Loire.

Grandmere was paralysed on one side of her body and

unable to communicate. She may have known who we were and I hope she did, for she looked intently at us when we arrived. So I talked to her, talked about all the years she lived in England with my grandfather, I talked about the summers I spent more recently in France, the work in the vineyard, staying with her in the chateau, the wonderful meals she prepared, my favourite dishes. I told her how happy I had been there and how grateful I was.

Throughout, she gazed at me, surely with understanding, and I felt she wanted to say something to me. But she never spoke and soon after she slipped into a coma. Two days later she was dead.

We stayed at the chateau for a few days after the funeral, helping with all the arrangements, dealing with visitors who called to see the family and keeping my uncle and aunt company.

The contents of the will came as a shock. My grandmother had married my grandfather, an English wine merchant, when she was in her early twenties and had lived with him in England until his death, some forty years later. Then she had returned to France with Martin, her elder son, and taken over the family business in partnership with her brother, now deceased. As the sole owner of the business, she had made provision for her son to live in the chateau for the rest of his life, but she had left the chateau and the vineyard jointly to him, married but without issue, a consequence, or so it was said, of his having mumps when he was a young man, and to her younger son, Benjamin, my father, and in the event that he predeceased her to his heir. Other assets such as money and shares were also to be divided between Uncle

Martin and, as my father's heir, myself. After my father's death she had presumably seen no reason to amend her will, so half of her considerable fortune passed to me. This amounted to more than half a million pounds, which I would receive within three months. I was also the owner of half a chateau and half a vineyard, which I could do nothing about without the agreement of my uncle, or until his death.

I was rich. Very rich. My future wealth was assured.

My uncle, a fairly wealthy man in his own right, kindly said that he would be prepared to run the business on his own, leaving me free to pursue my own interests, or to enter into an active working partnership with me, whichever I wanted. It was decided that these considerations were best left for the time being and that I would stay with him in the near future, which would be a more appropriate time to discuss business and family matters. Shortly after, my mother and I returned to England.

The inheritance helped to alleviate my grief for Grandmere. I know this may sound callous but I doubt if it is an uncommon reaction when relatives come into an unexpected fortune. I was upset when she died; I shed genuine tears at her funeral and if I could have brought her back I would have done. Although not overly close or demonstrative, she had always been kind to me and if she had noticed my nightly liaisons with Pierre, she turned a blind eye and tactfully asked no questions when she heard of the arrival of Krystina. She flew over, bringing a carrycot full of clothes and a cheque for £500 and stayed for a week.

Her death brought release for me. With heady excitement, I was ready and more than able to spread my wings, see the world and make my mark upon it. Where this ambition was to take me, I was not sure. The thought of taking up my studies again, as my mother suggested, seemed like long, protracted work and I didn't see the purpose. Not when I already owned, or co-owned a business, and had enough money to live, perhaps not in extravagant luxury but certainly without any financial worries. My opportunity was staring me in the face.

The demand for wine was growing, my father had predicted that wine sales in England would more than double within ten years. Port and lemon, Babycham, Dubonnet, were already passé and it was only a matter of time before sales of the cheap, indeterminate wines of the uninitiated, would decline. Young people were developing a taste for wine and they would become more discerning; it would no longer be a question of red or white, sweet or dry, but Chardonnay, Merlot, Sauvignon, Pinot Noir, Chenin, Burgundy, Sancerre. Wines would still be subjected to the pretentiousness of fashion and class, but to a much lesser degree; people's taste buds were often in their pocket. The future would be quality and value for money.

And here I was, already in the trade and knowing something about it. I had a lot more to learn, but I knew where I would be going.

My father had left my mother comfortably provided for. She owned the house, the mortgage had long since been paid, and she owned the shop and said she would continue running it for a few more years as my father would have done. Unlike my father she knew very little about wine, but she knew the price of every can or bottle, how many we had sold in a week and what profit had been made.

She irritated me much less now with her little clichéd sayings, her somewhat provincial attitude to life, for I recognized that she was a stable, sensible woman, her feet firmly rooted in daily reality with all its steadfastness and tedium. I must have added to her troubles over the past three or four years, but she had been good to me and I had relied utterly on her.

*

It was time for me to move out of the parental home and to move on. The world, as my mother said, was my oyster.

I handed in my notice at work and I left Nichols and Wilson a month later. I bought a car, a little larger, more powerful than strictly necessary, bright red. Diane went into raptures when she saw it. My mother merely said, 'It's very nice, Claire, it suits you.' Then she added, almost as an afterthought, 'Perhaps a touch flashy.' I planned to go to France in time for the grape-picking and to learn more about the business.

The grape picking began in late September and we were now in the last week of August. It was then that I thought I would go away on holiday. I didn't have to save up or wait for annual leave at work. I was footloose and fancy-free. And rich. And where else but Cornwall, where I had that idyllic family holiday all those years ago?

Memories from thirteen years ago surfaced in my mind and if you had asked me then when I had been happiest, I would have said during that glorious summer with both my parents, amidst sand and sea, cliffs and green rugged pathways.

I would find a place near the sea, get up late, read books, cook or eat out, swim each day, bask in the sun and take Krystina with me. She was a happy and good-natured child; Ricky's dark hair framed her pale, oval face giving it an elfin-like quality, she was endearingly lovely. I would have her all to myself. Just the two of us, together.

It was well into the holiday season, but I found a place almost immediately. There was a two bedroomed terrace house close to the sea, available for a month following a cancellation. I had planned for two weeks, but a month seemed an even better idea and I sent a cheque immediately to confirm the booking.

'Are you really sure you want to stay that long? After all, you're not used to looking after Krystina on your own, not for that length of time. She's a good little girl, but children can be a handful and you don't want to get too tired.' That was my mother, of course.

'I want to have some time alone with her, just the two of us. We'll be on holiday, able to do what we like. It will do her good and me too.'

My mother insisted that I take our own bed linen and a couple of sleeping bags and pillows, she thought it was more hygienic; you never knew what you might find in rented furnished accommodation. These, together with all our summer clothes, I packed in a very large holdall. It was the type of holdall used by mountaineers and it had belonged to my father who, as a young man, had been a keen and quite accomplished climber in the Alps. In later years, he used it whenever he drove to France, or other European countries on business and so, for me, it had sentimental value.

Krystina was excited as she sat in the car. 'Going to sea! Bye, bye, Gamma!'

'Have a nice holiday,' called Diane.

'Nice 'day. Going to sea,' she replied.

'Take care of yourselves,' said my mother who managed to look worried while blowing a kiss to Krystina. 'See you again, soon.'

'See soon,' Krystina said, waving goodbye. 'See soon.'

I drove away. It would be another five years before I saw my mother again and then I would return with two children and a husband.

5

Five years is a long time in a child's life and it was a long time in mine.

After the ill-fated month in Cornwall I drove straight to Southampton dragging a reluctant, protesting child with me. 'I want to go home!' was a recurring cry and she screamed when she saw the boats in the port. 'Not yet! Later! We must see Uncle Martin and Auntie Carla first!' I had to speak sharply to her a few times, before she became sullenly quiet and withdrawn. It was wrong of me to do so because earlier I had told her that we would be going home.

I could feel no pity for her as my own feelings were in turmoil, my hopes shattered. Fearful hidden forces seemed to pursue me and with a grim, savage determination to evade them, I drove the car on to the ferry.

By the time I drove off the ferry and into France, I knew, no matter how desperate my circumstances, how disconsolate I was, I had to get a grip on my own feelings and I had to be gentle, forbearing, steadfastly kind. I would patiently acclimatize her to a new way of life. I owed it to her. It was not her fault that I was dragging her away with me.

After driving for several hours we spent the night at a hotel. The new surroundings and the language upset her.

'Isn't this exciting? People here don't speak English, they speak French. The waiter didn't say, "Thank you" he said, "Merci". He said, "oui" instead of "yes", "oui"means "yes". Isn't that interesting? I can speak French and soon you will be able to speak French . Won't that be nice?'

'I don't want to,' she said.

She pushed her food around her plate and ate only three or four of the chips.

'In French chips are called "frites". You can remember that, can't you?'

So I prattled on, deliberately taking two or three days to reach the chateau, doing my best to help her to settle in a different country with a different language and to understand that we would not be there for long; it was only a holiday, we would be going home soon, but in the meantime she must be good and not complain. She remained unhappy and apathetic.

When we reached the Loire Valley I stopped the car a kilometer away to look down on the vineyard and the chateau. I remember it now: the subdued colours that blended together in the September sun, the warmth that seemed to come from the land itself and I even fancied the faint smell of grapes in the air pervading that safe and gentle landscape.

'Look!' I said, waving my hand across the view in front of us. 'Isn't this land beautiful? This is our home in France. This is our land. One day, when you grow up, it will all be yours!'

'I don't want it,' she said.

'Ah, Krystina!' Uncle Martin exclaimed, coming out of the chateau to greet us the moment we stepped out of the car in front of the door. He picked her up, holding her high above him. 'So you've come to see your Uncle Martin and Auntie Carla! The last time I saw you, you were just twelve months old. Now, my word! How you've grown! You're a big girl, now.'

'I want to go home,' she said.

'This is your home, your home in France.'

She looked around her, at the large house in front of her, uncomprehending, and began to cry.

'Here you are, my darling, Mummy's here, she hasn't gone away,' he said, handing her back to me. 'It must be strange for her, she's not used to us.'

'She's unsettled,' I said. 'She misses Mum very much and she hasn't been away before. She's been on a boat and come to a country where suddenly everyone speaks a language she doesn't understand. That seems to have really upset her. She's tired and confused.'

Later at dinner I said, 'I wanted to see you now because I've made up my mind. I really want to learn more about the business. I know only what Dad has taught me about wine – and that has been a bit limited when it comes to the business side of things, although, of course, it was useful, it gave me an insight. I need to learn much more and perhaps, eventually, and when Krystina is a bit older and I'm a bit wiser, we'll go into partnership as you suggested. It keeps it all in the family and I think Dad would approve, don't you?'

'He would be very proud of you, my dear; but then, he always was, you know.'

Uncle Martin smiled, a mixture of pride and sadness. 'I'm very glad. I … no, *we* had hoped you would decide on the partnership. Of course, there's no immediate hurry.'

'I'll spend most of my time here, just looking around

while the grape picking is underway,' I continued. 'Of course, I've seen this before, but now I can pay more attention and Krystina can come with me. It will be a new experience for her and she'll get used to hearing French. I want us to speak in French as much as possible. It will be good for her.'

Carla smiled but her tone of voice was serious. 'Don't rush things, Claire, she'll pick it up soon enough. She has to get used to the place. She's played around with her food tonight although she's eaten most of it, but she hasn't spoken a word throughout the meal.'

'Perhaps you're right. She'll be more communicative once she's settled down. I think she's tired, it's past her bedtime, she's usually in bed by half past seven. I'll warm some milk now. She has a drink of milk and honey at bedtime and drinks it while I'm reading her a story.'

I took her to the kitchen, heated the milk, added honey, and a small splash of whisky, then took her to bed. I didn't go down until she had fallen asleep.

I phoned my mother who was still annoyed that we had not gone home before going France.

'I really think you should have come home first, Claire. It's too much change for Krystina, too much excitement, all this travelling about. How long are you staying? And what about that boyfriend, the one you were telling me about?'

I felt sick. When I tried to speak my throat ached and the words were lost. I had phoned her from a phone box once a week while we were on holiday, because the house had no telephone. I had told her about the Goodmans taking us to the Tregeagle Inn, the children's play area, the pub lunches, the Disney film. She knew all about Mark, – handsome, clever, thoughtful, sensitive, amusing, wonderful with Krystina , lovely parents – oh, yes, I had sung his praises, with an enthusiasm I did not try to disguise.

'Claire?'

'Yes?'

'Well, what happened?'

I breathed deeply, tried to steady my voice. 'Nothing. I just thought, after a month's holiday, as planned, I needed to spend more time here, learning more about the business.'

'Will you see him again? … Mark, I mean?'

The ache in my voice tightened like a ligature. 'Possibly. We'll see what the future holds.'

'I see. Well, I'll phone in a couple of days, see how things are.'

I went to bed soon after, pleading tiredness, and cried for hours alongside a child who slept, but tossed and turned throughout the night. In the morning I had to be very firm with her. I told her she must stop complaining about being there and although she didn't remember them, Martin and Carla were *her* uncle and aunt as well as mine. She seemed to accept this but didn't respond. She sat still at the breakfast table, slowly eating food and gazing, somewhat trance-like, at nothing in particular, while I kept up a stream of conversation to fill the mute atmosphere which seemed to emanate from her.

Diane phoned the next day to say my mother was worried about me and then asked me about Mark.

'It's over, Diane. I'm O.K. as long as I keep busy and don't think about it and I can't talk about it, not even to you. Just reassure Mum, tell her I'm fine, you know what she's like.'

Diane told me to phone if ever I wanted a quiet chat and then talked about the shop and the current boyfriend.

She phoned again, about a week letter, to say a letter had arrived at the shop for me from Cornwall. Mark's name and address were on the back. I thought carefully for agonizing moments, before answering. Mark had never needed to know my address in Sussex, although he knew we had a shop in the town. He had obviously found the address of the off-license through Directory Enquiries.

My voice was surprisingly firm and detached when I spoke, 'Send it back, Diane. Cross out our address and write across the envelope: *Unwanted. Return to Sender.*'

'Good Heavens, Claire! Whatever happened? I had no idea something ....'

I cut in: 'Just do it, Diane! Get it in the post today. If he ever phones, say I went away and you cannot give a forwarding address. If pressed, just say I want no further contact with him.'

Diane's voice was subdued when she spoke. 'Claire, I'm so sorry, you must have had a terrible time. I really didn't know...'

'It's O.K. There's no need to worry about us. And, Diane, don't mention this to Mum, it will only upset her.'

'No, of course not. I'll get the letter off right away. Don't worry, I won't tell Christine.'

We were alone in the chateau at the time and after the phone call we went to the bedroom. I spread toys and books on the floor, then collapsed on the bed, feeling very sick and with the worst headache I had ever had.

We settled in the chateau better than I had anticipated, partly because my aunt and uncle, though loving and attentive enough, were not naturally effusive or overly inquisitive. They were in their sixties, their lives regulated by the seasons, the routine of the business and both were very busy at that time of year. On most days we met for breakfast and the evening meal, which suited me well.

Although I had difficulty sleeping at night, by day I could not rest. I was driven into action. I always had to be doing something, I had to keep going: to rest, to relax, would make me a prey to memory, a moment's loss of awareness or concentration could lead to disaster. When alone, I busied myself cleaning, tidying, preparing meals for when they returned. Each day I spent hours out of doors, walking and playing. 'She needs the exercise, the fresh air will do her good,' I said. I took her with me when I joined the workers to help with the vines. Many knew me already but few knew that I had a daughter.

'Bonjour, Krystina!' they would call and after a few days, encouraged by me, she began to respond.

'Bonjour,' she would answer timidly.

In the three months we were there she learnt four words, *bonjour, au revoir, oui, merci.* This was gratifying and I hugged her with lavish praise. She complained less, became a little more amenable, though quiet and pensive during the day and prone to tears at night.

It was Carla who gave me the opportunity to voice plans I had been formulating since I arrived in France.

'You know Christine is worried about you?' she said one evening while Uncle Martin was out.

I knew this. Every time she phoned, it was the same story.

'You should come home, Krystina needs more stability,

she isn't used to all this running around, you'll need to put her in a nursery or playgroup soon, she's two and a half now and needs to play with other children. Martin says you're hyperactive; it sounds to me as if you're living on your nerves, looking after her all on your own is too much for you, Claire, you're not used to it; you need to come back soon, there'll be plenty of time to work in the vineyard; why don't you come home for Christmas. Martin suggested that I come over for Christmas, but you know how busy we are in the shop then; perhaps later in January I could come over, if you really are intent on staying there that long, although I hope ... '

So it went on.

'I really need this time, Carla. I'm serious about the business, and I need time with Krystina. I know I'm over-protective but I do need to be the one who's responsible for her. So far, Mum and Diane have been with her more than I have.'

'But you are hyperactive, you don't stop. You are as thin as a rake, the weight is dropping off you. You need to ease up a bit, for your own sake and Krystina's. Perhaps you should go back home, just for a while, get some rest.'

'I need to be away from England. I can't go back, I can't face it. I have to go away, be on my own with her. It's for her sake as well as mine. I can't go back, not yet, I really can't.'

'It's because of this man, isn't it? The one you met in Cornwall?'

Tears sprang to my eyes and I could not speak.

'I thought so. Christine told me about him and I said to your uncle, "All this is to do with a man, she's running away from something." What is it?'

'Nothing,' I said sobbing and seconds passed before I could continue. 'Nothing. Just one of those things. It didn't work out.'

Carla understood, or thought she did. I was to get some rest, try to have a good night's sleep and we could talk about it the next day.

Again, as I half expected, it was the following evening, my uncle being present this time as well.

He began, 'Claire, Carla's been telling me you don't want to go back home, at least not for a little while.'

'Yes, Uncle, it would not be a good idea. I need time away.'

'You know, you can stay here. You can move in permanently, you and Krystina. I'm not sure what Christine would say about it, but it would be fine with us. In fact, we would like it if you decided to live here.'

'I do want to spend more time here, maybe permanently, but now is not the time. I'm twenty three and have lived at home for my entire life. I realized while we were on holiday in Cornwall that I'd like to go travelling for a while before I settle down properly in the business. A sort of gap-year, if you like, well, just for a few months. Even Mum shouldn't object to that. Just Krystina and me, together, on our own.'

'How long do you intend to stay away?'

'It depends. Maybe a few months.'

'And where would you go?'

'I think Australia, perhaps even New Zealand, would be the best places for both of us. It's what a lot of students do, usually before they go to university. There's no problem in getting in, everyone speaks English, a bit like home actually and plenty to see. It would be something new for me and, of course, I could visit the wineries there. I've read about them – they're amazing! That alone is reason enough to go to those countries. Then, there's Krystina. I really do appreciate this time I have alone with her.'

Uncle Martin seemed to weigh these words in his mind; he was concerned, there was doubt in his voice when he spoke. 'Well, you seem to have thought about it for a while.'

'Only recently. My life has changed and it's made me think of other possibilities.' I said no more as tears threatened like unwelcome guests.

Carla looked at me intently; then, turning to Uncle Martin, said softly, 'I think it's a good idea.'

'When did you think of going?'

'Well, it's almost summer in Australia now, so the weather will be good. Grape picking starts in February. I could take a look at the wineries. I'd like to find out more. Australian wine is getting a good reputation. The quality is there.'

Uncle Martin laughed. 'I must say, you're very enthusiastic about it! Don't get carried away. There's plenty of time to transform the wine industry. The French have been doing it for two hundred years.'

'Time doesn't stand still anywhere, least of all in the wine trade,' I said and, of course, Uncle Martin would have known this more than I did at the time.

France has a long history of the cultivation of grapevines, and an extensive knowledge of wine, but its world wide reputation has been steadily challenged over the years by its wine-making neighbours. Thousands of those Europeans, who emigrated over the last hundred years, took their skills and knowledge with them to lands far away, much bigger than their own countries and where soil and sun combined to produce grapes at least as lush and sweet as any they could find at home.

'Dad used to say the wines coming from the other side of the world would soon be our main competitors.'

'He was probably right. Ben always kept track of that side of the business, he could see things coming, while I just concentrated on production from one year to the next. I must say, some first hand experience of these places would be interesting, might even be useful, you never know.'

'Well, why don't we sleep over it?' Carla suggested. 'Let it all sink in a bit. See how you feel tomorrow.'

The following morning I overheard them talking in the kitchen before breakfast.

'It's a bit extreme isn't it? She's too restless. She's been on tenterhooks since she arrived, something's upsetting her, that's for sure.'

'Martin, I don't know what went wrong, but it's to do with that boy she met in Cornwall. She as good as admitted it the other night and Christine thinks the same. She doesn't know about the travelling plans yet.'

'And I wouldn't like to be the one to tell her. It won't go down well, you know.'

'Christine worries too much – and I'm not criticising, she's had much to worry about since Ben died, what with the shop and Claire and she's been like a mother to Krystina. But she's not the possessive type, she may even see that it makes sense. It gives Claire that bit of space and freedom she hasn't had. She needs to spend more time now with Krystina. The child's too quiet, she isn't all that secure, you can tell that. She needs to know who her mother is.'

I came in the breakfast room just then and they looked up and stopped talking.

'I heard you talking about me,' I said with a smile. 'I don't mind, especially as you seem to agree with me.'

They laughed and right then I felt something had been accomplished. My plans, so essential to me, might go ahead.

'I think it's a good idea,' Carla said enthusiastically. 'Get away from complications, negative memories. It's what I'd do myself, if I were in your situation. It will be a long holiday, a new start, good for both of you.'

It was as easy as that. It was more difficult with my mother.

'A long holiday? Going to the other side of the world! It's so sudden! And you sound quite … well, quite agitated about it. I don't know what's got into you!'

'I'm not agitated! I may sound excited because I really want to do this. It's the right thing to do and, above all, this is the right time to do it.'

'Frankly, I'm worried about Krystina, Claire. Martin said she had a tantrum the other night when you put her to bed and Carla thinks she's too quiet and a bit insecure. Children need more stability, it's too much change, too much excitement, for her.'

'Mum, she's all right. Of course she clings to me a bit, she's in a different country and it's strange for her and two is the age for tantrums. She's had two, one in Cornwall and one here, neither too extreme nor long lasting. Compared to some children, she's letting me off lightly.' I laughed to show I was relaxed about it and to reassure her. 'We go out each day. The workers are always talking to her even if she doesn't understand what they say, but she answers, just a couple of words in French. I think she's enjoying it. She's doing very well considering how different it is here.'

'Well, I think you should come home for a while before going off again.'

'That will upset her more. Right now, she thinks we are still on holiday and everything we're doing is part of this big adventure and she's coping well with it. I've been too selfish in letting you do so much.'

'No, no, I really don't mind. I was glad to help, you mustn't think …'

'Mum, listen to me,' I interrupted. 'I couldn't have managed without you. But you need a break from both of us, time to see more people, like you used to do, time to lead more of your own life. It's time I took full responsibility for her. This is the right time for both of us to make a fresh start.'

My mother was not immune to this reasoning, there was a somewhat reluctant acceptance, but she said she could understand the way I felt. So I moved the conversation on to the business and talked about the quality of the grapes this year, the number of workers, how much wine we had made the previous year, how much we had sold.

I told her that it had been a good year for the grapes, the wine would keep its *Vin délimité de Qualité,* but I was concerned about the cost of production. It would not be able to compete with some of the cheaper new wines coming on the market. Only the top French wines, those with the *A.C.* ratings were likely to make a good profit and soon we would have to find a way of being more competitive.

My mother listened and said she thought I was using my

time there very well. Yet I was only saying what my father had already predicted about the family wine years ago.

'Eastern European wines are already popular, reasonably good, middle of the range, but at much lower prices. Of course, labour is cheaper. The real competition is Australia, land is cheaper there. They have good grapes and European immigrants who know what they're talking about when it comes to wine. In twenty years they may be serious competitors.'

'I wouldn't have thought that was likely; anyway, the chateau wine is mainly sold in France, isn't it?'

'Well, yes and no. It will keep the market locally although we're not the only chateau in the area and we really need to increase our exports if we are to keep the business seriously profitable.'

'But you won't stay away for too long, will you?'

'Oh, I'm thinking of an antipodean summer,' I said, my voice breaking. I composed myself quickly, took a deep breath and continued with as much cheeriness as I could muster, 'Just think, we'll miss winter and by the time we come back, we'll be ready for a second summer. There's no time like the present and Uncle Martin agrees with me. The best research is done on the ground, he says. Anyway, it's cold here now, and it will be even colder at home. Krystina needs more sunshine anyway and we'll be going straight into summer and missing a European winter.'

The following evening she phoned and had a long chat with Uncle Martin. Just before he called me to the phone to speak to her, I heard him say, 'Don't worry, it will do her the world of good. She's leaving the car here so she's not likely to be away for long, is she?'

It seemed that Martin's approval had been necessary for her. She said she wasn't entirely happy with the idea but perhaps I was right, she would get used to it. I knew she had when she started to warn me about the dangers of travelling, arriving in places late at night without pre-booked accommodation, of uncooked food, tap water, upset tummies and pickpockets. As I listened patiently I contemplated the years ahead with a glimmer of optimism, like warm sun in winter, before we ended the call in friendly agreement.

I put the phone down and wept, tormented with regret, yet suddenly energised with relief and hope like one who has just been reprieved from a life sentence.

Two weeks later we were on our way to Australia.

6

On the long flight to Australia, I began to relax a little. A child's first experience of a long flight produces either restless excitement or boredom and fatigue; the novelty can soon wear off. She was tearful and I tried to divert her with fairy stories, funny poems, snap, colouring books, but her concentration and enthusiasm lasted only for a few minutes; she slept on and off for much of the journey. I was grateful for a relatively unremarkable and peaceful journey and only too glad to get as far away from Cornwall as possible.

Those early years in Australia were fraught with acute misery; worry, sadness and despondency seemed to afflict both of us in equal measure. The feelings of adult and child are transmitted from one to the other when they are in such close proximity, day after unremitting day. Night offered only limited release for both of us: she slept, but tossed and turned; I slept little and when I did I was soon wakened by dreams that tormented me nightly.

I handled the situation as best I could, trying to establish some sort of routine in her life and treating her with firmness and kindness. Yes, I was firm, very firm at times, but I was also patient and kind. I never faltered. It was a difficult time for both of us, but I had no option but to be resolute.

After a month in Sydney, visiting all that Sydney had to offer – the Harbour Bridge, the Opera House, Bondi Beach, ferry-hopping from one island to the other, searching for kangaroos and koalas, and spending some time in the Blue Mountains – we travelled to Adelaide and I rented a small apartment in the Barossa Valley, the main wine producing area in the country. We visited the surrounding wineries and I soon became known at two or three of them, for I made a point of chatting to the workers, some of whom were descended from the German families who had emigrated there the previous century.

One day, as I was in the shop where tourists and other visitors came to buy the wine, one of the assistants introduced me to the manager.

'This is Claire Moreton, the English visitor I was telling you about,' she said to Tony Merkel, the manager.

Tony asked me questions about the family vineyard and was impressed when he knew I was part owner. He invited me into the tasting room and asked for my opinion of the wine he had there. I was not a professional wine taster by any means, but even when I was quite young my father had always made me taste the family wine with great care: 'Swirl it round the glass … just a little … smell it … take your time … taste … just a little … concentrate … think … what can you taste?' In such matters a little knowledge and a reasonably sensitive palate are all that is necessary. A confident manner does the rest.

He offered me four of the reds. Common sense tells you,

if you are being tested, no matter how informally, that they are likely to include a range of quality, besides, I already had a good idea of their grapes and wine production.

'Young, … last year's, most likely, … light body.'

'A bit rough, this one. Either too many stalks were left on or too much press juice was added, probably the latter. There's a harsh tannic taste which overpowers the mellowness of the fruit – what is it – sort of mushy plum?'

'This one is lovely, fruity, light. Cabernet Sauvignon? Merlot? Probably mixed. Very pleasant wine, probably good value as well.'

'This is as good as anything we've produced back home, maybe better. Rich, full of flavour. At least thirteen percent, I imagine. A dearer wine, of course, – it needs to be.'

Tony Merkel was suitably impressed. 'I don't know how long you're staying in the area but would you be interested in working here? A couple of days a week, even a half day or two would help. We're a bit short staffed in the shop at the moment.'

'I'll need to bring my daughter with me,' I said, 'she won't be any trouble, she's rather quiet and shy.'

'If you're happy with that, then it's fine by me. There's a garden with a swing next to the shop, a table and a sofa in the staff room, she can bring her toys, crayons and things. Feel free to wander round the place as much as you like. Make yourself at home.'

It was just what I needed and we settled on a modest fee for my services, which involved either serving people in the shop or accompanying them on tours of the vineyard.

I spent five half days a week at the winery and stayed for

three months. The work gave me something to concentrate on, to take my mind, however temporarily, off other things. I read, observed, discussed and crammed my head with the history and science of wine production; facts and figures were recorded with detailed notes in labeled files, which began to bulge with information. This obsessive immersion in work offered timely relief, if only for a few hours out of long days and dream-filled nights. It kept me sane.

Periodically, I sent detailed reports back to my uncle and my mother, all designed to impress them with the knowledge I had acquired about the type of grapes, the type of soil, the weather, the methods of production, the picking, fermentation, pressing, maturing, fining and bottling; the mechanization, the size of the workforce, the labour costs, the sales, the exports and the marketing .

This was of little practical importance to Uncle Martin but he was interested and responded well to my dedication and enthusiasm, while my mother declared herself impressed and delighted in the letters she sent, which often ended with comments such as, 'You seem to be a learning a lot' and 'I'm glad you are using your time so well' and once, 'I must admit, this is a very good experience for you and for Krystina as well, she's seeing new things, meeting new people and it's good that she's still near you while you're working.'

My mother always wanted to speak to her when she phoned and I sometimes made excuses saying she was asleep; I so dreaded my mother hearing her plaintive voice saying, 'Can I go home now?' However, with some encouragement and prompting from me, she started to answer questions with a yes or a no, and within two or three months she would say where she had been that day and my mother soon began to marvel at how many words she now knew and how she seemed to be acquiring an Australian accent.

She spent her days trudging along with me as we went to the market or the park and, once, to Kangaroo Island. When people spoke to her she would answer, simple answers of one or two words. We often went to the swimming pool, where she sometimes played with other children and I taught her to swim. She loved the water and was usually the youngest swimmer in the pool, most other children of her age were still wearing armbands.

We stayed in the Barossa Valley area for four months and then from Adelaide we went to Ayer's Rock, as it was known then, before it, once more, became Uluru, and spent a week in Alice Springs before going on to Darwin. It was important to keep moving.

Both my mother and my uncle kept all the postcards we sent while I was away. I packed as much information about each place we stayed in as I could, filling the spaces with almost microscopic writing. I have them still, cheerful postcards to let everyone know we were having a wonderful time, signed with a flourish, accompanied by a childish scrawly K. It was far from a wonderful time, but with each week that passed the many new and diverting sights brought new experiences crowding out older memories.

We followed the well-beaten tourist track in that huge country – Cairns, the Coral Sea, Brisbane, Sydney, the Blue Mountains, Melbourne, doing all the things that tourists do, but the following January, having been in Australia for over a year, we stopped for a while in the Swan and Hunter Valleys.

We went from one winery to the next, observing the scale and breadth of the industry and chatting to the many workers who descended on the area at that time. I duly reported back to my mother and Uncle Martin, making some comments, even suggestions about mechanization processes.

Later in the year I concentrated on the smaller, family-owned wineries which are typical in Victoria and which, perhaps, most closely resemble our own in France. The wine was often sold locally, from the winery itself. Its reds, from the spicy Shiraz to the full-bodied Cabernet, were modestly impressive, and could be produced more cheaply than our own.

My mother's letters and phone calls became more frequent and insistent. When were we coming home? A holiday was one thing but two years amounted to emigration. Did I intend to emigrate?

'Of course not,' I said, although it had crossed my mind. 'My visa's been extended, I can stay here because I can support us both. We are having a wonderful time, I am learning so much and …'

'Do you think it's good for Krystina being away for so long? She will forget who we are soon, if she hasn't already.'

'Mum, I should have done this years ago on my own. Then I wouldn't have made so many mistakes in my life. As for Krystina, I really think she's benefiting from the experience as much as I am and it's good for us to be together, I can give her plenty of attention. This is her opportunity as well as mine, you know, and we won't be able to do this once she starts school and she's seeing so much, doing so well here. I thought we may pop across to New Zealand before coming back…'

'New Zealand!'

'Well, it makes sense, you know. And while we are here we may as well …'

'I really don't know what's got into you. It's madness, traipsing around with a young child like that …'

I let her ramble on and when she finally stopped, I merely said, 'I've considered that already, because I knew you would say it. And after such consideration, I've made my decision. We're going.'

'Very well, then. If you won't see sense, so be it.'

We ended the call slightly frosty but polite enough.

7

We left from Melbourne and flew to Christchurch where I rented an apartment and found a suitable school. The thought of being separated from her worried me enormously and I agonized over this decision, but she was five years old and needed to mix with other children. Despite our continual travelling from one place to another, I had tried to keep to a fairly strict routine. Early mornings and evenings, wherever we were, had been spent together on various activities. I had spent hours talking and playing games and teaching her the alphabet so she could read a little and do simple arithmetic.

'Krystina is very advanced for her age,' said Miss Kelly, the teacher who ran the school. 'She's a bright little girl, very well behaved. She has settled in quite well, although socially she's rather shy, a little withdrawn.'

'We have done a lot of travelling so she hasn't had so much opportunity to mix with friends of her own age,' I said.

'Oh, I do understand. It will take her a little time to get used to us and we will do our best to encourage her to participate in group activities. She has told us once or twice that she is going home soon but she seems unsure where that is. We don't know if she means here with you or going back to England.'

This was true. She no longer wanted to go home, but she was aware that there was another home, somewhere far way. She knew Grandma, whom she spoke to on the phone twice a month, lived there and that, one day, we would be going back. 'Soon, one day, soon,' I would always say.

'Wherever we are staying tends to become home for a while and we've stayed in so many places. We have a home in France where my uncle and aunt live. She talks mostly about our home in England, my mother looked after her there and she talks a lot about her.'

Miss Kelly was satisfied and soon after I invited other children around to our rented apartment and I made friends with their mothers. In this way I began to have more of a social life myself. I decided that we would make our home here for several months, perhaps a year. It would provide stability.

Some four months later Miss Kelly reported, 'We can see a huge improvement in Krystina's social skills. She talks more and she's making friends with other children. She seems to enjoy being here.'

I had noticed the improvement. She was easier to handle, slept better, often told me what she had done at school each day before I asked. She was more at ease with everyone, including me.

At weekends we would sometimes get together with friends, or drive to various places of interest in the South Island, the Paparoa and Westland National Parks, Arthur's Pass, Lake Tekapo, Mount Hutt, Hammer Springs, Kaikura and the wineries. The pace of life was slower, the people relaxed and peaceful, the scenery spectacular. It was a pleasant, easier life.

The wine industry in New Zealand did not, at that time, match Australia's and although there were some large wineries, many were very small, much smaller than our own in France. They needed more development and were yet to profit from the end of restrictive protective practices. Although, in the trade, New Zealand wine was still, rather snobbishly, dismissed as plonk, I could see, and taste, the great potential in the promising Chardonnay, Sauvignon Blanc, Cabernet Sauvignon, Merlot and even the Pinot Noir, a somewhat difficult wine at times, and I knew then that within twenty years the reputation of New Zealand wine would rise significantly.

My written reports, carefully detailed, sent back to England and France continued to please and convince my family that, while I was having a long and adventurous holiday with a taste of freedom which only those with money can buy, I was also working and learning and showing a genuine commitment to our business interests.

At this time, I unexpectedly, put some of my business skills to use. I was talking to Elspeth Rogers, the co-owner of one of the new, small wineries in the Waipura district, who complained about some of the problems they were facing.

'The shops tend to buy in bulk, from the suppliers. The wine here isn't bad at all, but it can't compete with the expensive stuff and, as a cheaper wine, I don't make enough to satisfy the middlemen. They want high quality or high quantity. I'm stuck in the middle.'

I asked if I could taste some of her wine and then gave my verdict for what it was worth. 'Tannin is a bit strong in this one … this one is too early … you can do something about these next year. Most are decent enough table wines … cheaper end of the market certainly, but not the bottom end … not nasty cheap plonk … pleasant taste with subtle notes … good, everyday wines.'

'That's all very well,' she said ruefully, 'but people around here don't drink wine every day and those who are used to that sort of thing want something better.'

'Not necessarily,' I said. 'As an ordinary table wine this is quite acceptable. Those who don't drink much wine, perhaps only at birthdays, work parties and such like, are not experts, they don't want to pay too much and they should be quite happy with this.'

I put down the glass I had been sipping from and turned to her. 'You have a huge barn over there which is full of old furniture and rubbish.'

'Yes, we haven't got round to clearing it out.'

'Well, why don't you sell your wine direct, at least some of it, cut out the middleman, let people come to you, the local wine for local people.'

She thought about this for a while then said, 'But that sort of thing is for the larger wineries, ours is a very small business. In time, perhaps, when we're a bigger concern, perhaps, if we ever get that far.'

'You are only three miles from the nearest town, population about three thousand, and twenty miles from the next town which is much bigger. Promote it as an introduction to local wine. It shouldn't cost too much, you've got the building already.'

'It's a possibility, I suppose. We could afford it, if it worked. But we are very busy with the business and I don't see how …'

'Tell me how much you would pay to have it done and I'll do it for you.'

That is how I got the barn cleared, cleaned and painted, carpenter in, shelves put up, a counter for tasting and an area with chairs and tables. New wine labels with descriptions of each wine on them were printed; most wine labels at the time assumed that people knew what the wine they bought was supposed to taste like. An information display covered the whole of one wall with pictures of the wine process, from the planting of the vines to the wine at the table. Finally, leaflets were distributed throughout the town. The wine was sold for 25% less than it could be bought in the shop and six bottles could be bought at one time for the price of five.

The work took two months to complete and was within budget, so I made a small profit. It opened with about 100 people turning up on the first day and the local newspaper added to the publicity. There was a photo of Elspeth, her husband and me on the front page with the heading:

BUY LOCAL AND TASTE BEFORE YOU BUY

I was given credit for this local innovation:

> *Transforming the barn into an on-site wine store where visitors can roam around, read about the different wines, and taste before they buy was the brain child of Miss Claire Moreton, the English wine connoisseur.*

Connoisseur was pushing it a bit but I was pleased: this was yet another opportunity to show the family at home that I was doing something serious and a copy of the paper was sent home.

'Was that Krystina by the counter in the background?' my mother asked.

'Yes, she was at the opening ceremony; even had a sip of champagne, well, the house bubbly, actually.'

'I thought so. How she has grown! I really long to see her.'

I had sent the occasional snapshot of us during our travels, holding a koala, standing near a kangaroo, swimming in the deep end of the pool, playing with other children, enjoying the hot weather at Christmas in shorts and t shirts, sunhats and sunglasses, all carefully chosen.

I knew my mother enjoyed meeting up with old friends at home and was coping well enough without us, but she still kept pestering me to return, even hinting that she might come and visit us although that was unlikely for, apart from the fact that she didn't like travelling, she felt she could not leave the shop in the hands of the three shop assistants, for more than a few days. Since my father's death, she had never spent more than one week away from home, even when she went to France.

'Claire, you are managing all right, just the two of you, aren't you? You always used to sound a bit keyed-up and I wondered if Krystina ... '

'Mum, it's fine. She loves it here. She has adapted well, she likes living here. We are getting on well,' I said, although inwardly I was more hopeful than confident.

But the day came when that was how I truly felt.

★

It was in Christchurch, one day about six months after we arrived, that I was late picking her up from school. Usually, I arrived early, I was always the first parent there. On this particular day I had been delayed by road works, which held up the traffic for a short while. I parked the car and hurried up to the school five minutes after other children had been collected.

I heard her screams, piercing and frantic, before I reached the school gate and ran into the playground. Two teachers and a parent were standing around her, obviously concerned and trying to calm her while she screamed, her face stricken with panic.

I called, 'Krystina, I'm here! I'm here!' and when the teachers saw me they let her go and she looked up, broke away from them and ran headlong towards me, shouting, 'Mummy! Mummy! Mummy!'

I knelt down as she reached me and she fell into my arms crying, 'I thought you were gone! I thought you weren't coming back again! I thought you left me, you left me, you left me!' She sobbed uncontrollably and I could feel her heart beating very fast through her dress as she trembled in my arms.

I held her close to me. 'I was late, that's all. I didn't leave you. I'm not going away.'

At that moment I was only conscious of the child in my arms. She clung to me, as I clung to her. I felt my own heart beating, steadily, emphatically, within me.

'It's all right, Krystina. Mummy is here. I'll always be here. I'll never leave you.' She continued to sob but more quietly as the teachers hurried towards us.

'We don't know what happened! As soon as she saw you weren't there, she became hysterical. She seemed to think that you had left her and you weren't coming back. We tried to reassure her, said you'd be here soon, but it was no use, we couldn't calm her down.'

They were solicitous, asked us if we would like to come in, sit down, have something to drink, but I said we were fine. She had stopped crying and I wiped her face with a handkerchief and hugged her. I saw the fear change to worry, then to relief and as she held on to me, her little hands tightly holding on to my arms, I felt her complete acceptance of me, her need for me above all others and I knew from that moment, she was mine. I felt a sudden surge of love for her which left me shaken and close to tears.

We spent the rest of the day, as usual, together, and I gave her constant attention and reassurance. We watched television together, way past her usual bedtime and we went to bed together. She always slept with me, but that night it was she who snuggled up and put her arm around me before falling asleep. She looked content, more at ease now, breathing slowly, rhythmically, as she peacefully slept. I lay awake for a long time, and let silent tears fall like soothing raindrops down my face and on to the pillow, which was still damp when I woke in the morning after a dreamless night.

The tide had turned and taken fear and rejection with it. I felt newly born; we were together, inseparable.

I thought often about going home at this time, but as I gazed at her, saw how well she was growing, how much more relaxed and confident she was becoming, I knew the time was not yet right. It would be another year or two, perhaps, before we were ready to return. Another year or two arguing with my mother. It would be difficult.

Help arrived, unexpectedly, in the form of Jeff Bentley. It was one of those rare coincidences when a benign fate gives a helpful hand in bringing two people who needed each other together.

Jeff was a marine biologist working for a government environmental agency in England and was offered a three year assignment to lead a research team at a university in New Zealand. It was a prestigious appointment and an exciting opportunity for him. He had been married for five years, but his wife, who had applied for and been offered a school teaching job there, refused to go, just one month before their planned departure, choosing instead to remain with her lover of two years. The news of the affair and the abrupt change in circumstances, so publicly evident, was shattering for Jeff, a thoughtful, modest man, whose own sense of honesty and loyalty was so deeply embedded in his fundamental decency that he could scarcely imagine it absent in those he loved.

He left England, divorce proceedings agreed and processed, and immersed himself in work, taking full advantage of his proximity to the Marlborough Sounds, one of the finest eco systems in the world. To this end, he travelled frequently from Wellington in the North Island to Picton in the South.

After a year of unremitting work, and the first substantial fall of snow that year, he decided to take a break. I, too, had decided to take advantage of the snow, and after packing our skis and clothes in the car we headed for Queenstown.

If the cable car had been full of people, as it usually was, it is unlikely that he would ever have spoken to us. But at that time, that day, we had found ourselves alone, just the three of us, sharing the cable car, which would take us up to the chair lift on the mountain.

He had spoken first. 'You're very young. Can you ski already?'

'Only on a small slope.'

'What's your name?'

'Krystina.'

'That's a nice name. How old are you?'

'Five.'

He turned to me and said he wished he had learned to ski when he was a child. 'I never put on a pair of skis until I was thirty and I'm still very clumsy, not really used to it. I'm better at swimming – I'm more at home in water.'

I said I learnt to ski in France when I was a child and Krystina was learning to ski now. I told him we went swimming in the summer, I thought it was important for children to swim as early as possible.

'I can swim in the sea and I can swim in the swimming pool – a whole length – all the way across.'

'That's very good. You can swim and ski. You're a clever girl, Krystina.'

Her face lit up and she smiled at him, pleased with this praise.

We left the chairlift, said goodbye and went our separate ways. It was several hours later and we were eating in the self service restaurant, when he came in, chose his food, paid for it and looked around for a table. He saw us and walked towards us.

'Hello, again. Have you had a good day?'

'It's been lovely. The snow was perfect. How about you?'

'Good! I only fell over twice. I'm quite pleased with myself. Did you do a lot of skiing, Krystina?'

'Yes, for a long time and I never fell over! I'm hungry now.'

'Well, I'll leave you to eat your food.' He turned to go, looking around for a table.

There were just the two of us sitting at a table for four. 'You can sit here, if you like. Krystina will be glad to have someone to show off to.'

He laughed and sat down with a smile which suggested that the invitation was what he had hoped for.

So began my friendship with Jeff Bentley.

Jeff was in Queenstown for the rest of the week and I extended my stay there for a few days so we spent the time skiing and we ate together in the evenings. He was an easy man to get along with, mildly humorous, attentive and considerate to both of us, not unattractive and quite distinguished in his field of work. In fact, he made a favorable impression both in manner and appearance.

I told him we had yet to visit Westland National Park, skiing was the best way to experience the glaciers there. After that we planned to go to the North Island where I intended to enroll on a short Business Studies course and place Krystina in a school.

'You will let me know when you return to the North Island, won't you? The moment you arrive in Wellington, you'll phone me, won't you? Promise?'

'Yes, yes, of course I will.'

'You'll remind her, won't you, Krystina? As soon as you get off the ferry, what are you going to say?'

'Phone Jeff.'

'That's right! Good girl!'

We said our goodbyes. Jeff returned to Wellington and we continued our journey in the South Island, skiing and sightseeing and, dutifully, I sent postcards and snaps of us home.

We took the ferry to the North Island two weeks later and we phoned Jeff from Wellington. He invited us to stay with him, we could have the spare bedroom, until we found a place of our own.

Krystina was captivated. She loved the attention he gave her, there was someone else to talk to, someone who showed her amazing pictures and specimens to do with his work and she became more involved with the mysteries of the beach and the sea. She began to draw and paint pictures of what she had seen on the beach and in the sea and this interest developed into a hobby which she still enjoys to this day, whenever she's not too preoccupied with work.

I realized early on that this man could give both of us all that we needed. We had arrived in his life when he was still recovering from an emotional upheaval and we offered him a new life, a family, a chance to start over again. He loved Krystina and he fell in love with me.

Six months later I married him.

Did I love him? Not as I had loved Mark, but I liked and admired Jeff. My fondness for him was close to love. It was enough. Many a marriage has been based on much less and ours was more than satisfactory. I never had reason to regret it.

In the early days of my marriage the dreams, which had become less frequent, returned, at least once or twice a week. I knew I was dreaming when I saw Mark running across the beach towards me as I stood motionless beside rocks, and I would hear myself struggling with the words, 'Wake up, wake up!' before I woke, writhing in the bed. At other times I would be flying across the beach myself, as if I were in a camera zooming at high speed towards the rocks and just as I thought I would crash into obliteration my flight would stop at one large, flat, white rock, still warm from the heat of the day, the rock crystals sparkling in the late afternoon sun, and I would wake, drenched in sweat, my heart beating wildly. Jeff comforted me, soothing me with soft words, 'It's only a dream … a dream … nothing to worry about.' I told him I had suffered from these 'mad nightmares of monsters' for five years, since I was in hospital.

The marriage was a perfect reason for us to stay longer in New Zealand and when I became pregnant a few months later I used the pregnancy to defer travelling saying I did not feel I was up for a long flight in my condition. In fact, I felt well; Jeff provided us with the security we needed, Krystina was happy, a normal, well-adjusted little girl, doing well at school. As the pregnancy progressed my fears and the nightmares diminished, and by the time James was born they had evaporated into the past.

We finally went home when James was four months old and Krystina was seven. I had been anxious about meeting my mother. She was over sixty but looked younger than when I had left. Mornings were spent in the shop, but she frequently left the late afternoons and evenings to the two assistants. Friends, the Women's Institute and the theatre took up her leisure time and it was clear that her life had moved on since I left. I was relieved and happy for her.

She liked Jeff immediately and later told me I had made a good choice and she was glad I had been sensible for once. She picked James up, declaring that he was the most amazing baby, so active, so observant of all that was going on, and decided that he looked like me.

However, it was on Krystina that her gaze lingered most; she looked at her in wonderment, searching for the child she knew five years ago, while recognizing that a child of seven is merely an approximation of herself at two; size, looks, manner and verbal communication, have changed with age and experience and these charges are reflected in the child's personality.

'I don't expect you remember me, do you, Krystina?'

'I remember you used to take me to the beach, before I learnt to swim.'

My heart seemed to jolt and my mother looked puzzled, but before she could speak I quickly said, 'That day we went to Brighton – don't you remember? All those pebbles on the beach, she brought some home with her.'

'Of course! I remember now. It's the only time we went to the beach. Fancy remembering that!' She turned, beaming with happiness, to Krystina, 'You were just two at the time. What a good memory you have!'

My mother showed her the photographs she had, talking about each one, then all the postcards we had sent from New Zealand and Australia. Later, as they walked hand in hand in the garden I began to relax. All would be well between them, my mother would take up the relationship where she left off and soon the five year gap would be nothing more than a blip in time.

'I can't believe how much she has grown!' my mother said later that evening. 'She has changed so much, so serious, so grownup. Her hair is lovely, so dark and glossy, and so long, it suits her. Remember the trouble we used to have washing it? She couldn't stand the water going over her head. And now she can swim, swim like a fish, Jeff said.'

Over the next few days she would spend minutes at a time gazing, first at one child, then the other. She looked at old photographs of me and of Krystina when we were babies and compared them with recent ones of James. 'Yes, he reminds me of you when you were a baby, same hair, same shape of head. Look, you can see the likeness.' And when Jeff was out of the room, 'I was never sure who Krystina looked like, but she's getting to look more like her father now, I think.' 'Yes,' I said, 'I've noticed, too. It's the eyes and the hair.' 'Well, I remember thinking he was a nice looking lad at the time. She's so well behaved, very polite, she's a credit to you. I already feel I'm getting to know her again.'

The homecoming was much easier than I had feared. Now there were four of us, a complete family, claiming the attention of my mother, then my uncle and aunt, who came over from France to see us. Within days, Diane, newly married, came with her husband and so did the many friends and faraway relatives who visited in an atmosphere of curiosity and excitement, the tribute paid to the new arrivals and the prodigal daughter.

My self-imposed exile was over.

The sense of relief I felt was commensurate with the

happiness of returning with a loving family and living a normal life in secure and fortunate conditions. We settled in a Sussex village, only twenty miles from the large town where I had grown up. It was a convenient place for both of us: Jeff travelled to various parts of the country and it was easy for me to fly or drive to France and, as I took on more of the responsibilities of running the business, I spent a good part of each year there.

Most of the school holidays were spent in France and Jeff often came with us, writing his reports there. Our children flourished. They had supportive, loving parents; we gave them opportunities many could not afford and they have made good use of them. They are considerate, caring and generous, both of them.

James is running the business with me now and I am increasingly in demand as a wine consultant, giving advice to small businesses and speaking at conferences.

I am a very wealthy woman and I know full well the value of money, its evils and its virtues. On balance, I have used my wealth wisely, both in business and within the family. I support various humanitarian causes, both at home and abroad, particularly those concerning disadvantaged children. The annual village fete, which I help to run, raises several thousands each year for the NSPCC. I am fortunate enough to have the means to help those in need and I consider it both a duty and a privilege to do so.

My mother, uncle, aunt and Jeff have succumbed to age and illness, a natural fate which awaits us all. I am now in my early fifties so, in normal circumstances, would expect to have many years ahead of me; my children are young adults, successful and independent; we are close, perhaps closer than ever. Family is everything to me: Krystina and James are my life.

★

This is my story.

I tell it because I need to be understood and we cannot understand anyone unless we know something of their past, for the past shapes us, makes us what we are. At times, it controls us. We can only try to understand others if we walk in their shoes, see through their eyes, listen to their words.

My story is close to the truth. Many could verify it, all who know me would believe it. It is the one I would like remembered, the one that does least harm.

But it is not complete.

The story we tell about ourselves depends on the time and place of disclosure, on our consideration for those who may be troubled by certain revelations. Above all, it depends upon our own needs, our own sense of worth. We are all prone to omissions and deceptions. We are reluctant to disclose our private thoughts and those actions which reveal too much about ourselves, we need hidden skeletons to remain buried. I have zealously concealed mine for thirty years to protect others and avoid my own ruin.

But recent events, like avenging spirits seeking retribution, have overtaken me. Now I have little choice, so I must press on.

PART TWO

8

'So, you are here! I can hardly believe it after all that palaver about not coming!' Krystina greeted me with a kiss as I stepped out of the car in front of the cottage.

'You wore me down. I had to give in,' I said, hugging her.

'You won't regret it, it's lovely here.'

She carried my case into the cottage. The table was laid ready for a meal for four and, indeed, I looked forward to it. Krystina is a good cook and I was hungry after the long drive.

'James and Anna will be back any minute. They went for a walk. I'll show you to your room and you can unpack and get sorted. By then, I'll have a gin and tonic ready.'

While we were sitting on the veranda which led out of the living room, drinking our gin and tonics, James and Anna arrived and there were the usual exclamations of delight expressed whenever the four of us meet after an absence, in this case of only two or three months. Brother and sister adore each other and we are, and always have been, a close-knit family. Krystina and James are conscious of my relatively new state of widowhood and phone me often, visit me more frequently; I know they talk together about what they can do to help, how well they think I am coping.

I do miss Jeff and I had hoped, even after the alarming

diagnosis, that he would respond well to treatment and perhaps go on for another ten years or so. As it was, the malignancy was particularly virulent and two years after the diagnosis he died. Jeff was twelve years older than I, a man who looked younger than his age, right up to three months before his death when cancer ravished his body and added ten years to his sixty five. Although severely weakened, his strong voice reduced to a frail whisper, his mind remained the same and he was patient, kind and considerate to the end. I remember him with devotion and gratitude, for my life would have been very different without him, but I am coping with widowhood.

Dinner that evening consisted of sole, fresh from Newlyn that morning, with capers and lemon, and small, lightly breadcrumbed croquettes of broccoli and potato, followed by thunder and lightning, that lovely mix of ice cream, gin and black treacle with a dollop of Cornish cream on top. Krystina is becoming intoxicated with all things Cornish.

'I love it here,' she said. 'I'm thinking of getting a place, a flat or something, just for a couple of months a year, a long weekend now and then, that sort of thing, we can all make use of it.'

'But it is so far away,' I said, "you would get bored living here and it's not practical for work.'

'I can see the attraction,' said James, 'but think how long it takes to get to London, even to France. What about work?'

'I can get on with some of my research here. I'm used to travelling. There are roads and trains and the internet, you know.' She smiled indulgently at us. 'It's not that far away and there's more going on here than you think. I love the space, the sea, the light … '

'Oh, show her your painting!' exclaimed Anna. 'It's ever so good. Show it to her, Krys.'

Krystina often paints when she is on holiday, she says she finds it relaxing. She fetched the painting and handed it to me. It was a beach scene, skillfully done, bright and alive with children playing on the sand and in the water. Shorts, swimming costumes, sundresses were painted in the brightest reds, pinks, yellows, dark blues and the towels and beach bags dotted here and there were in violet, indigo, burnt orange, glaring white. A calm ultramarine sea stretched back to meet an equally calm light blue sky at the horizon, becoming darker as it rose to the top of the paper. Sky and sea gave an impression of a benign tranquility. In contrast, the children, so brightly clad, displayed hyperactive exuberance. There was some inherent contradiction that made me feel uneasy.

'I started it the day we arrived,' she said. 'It was a lovely day, we were on the beach, it was just full of children playing. I finished it yesterday. I want to get this one framed. I'll keep it in my office, it will make the wall more interesting.'

'You've done the sand well,' I said, 'it looks like real sand.'

'A pale yellow sponge wash, sprinkled with salt. When it dried, I brushed the salt off, then gave it a thin coat of raw sienna with a toothbrush and the merest touch of burnt sienna for the sand near the water.'

We spent a few minutes discussing and praising the painting.

'This is the first painting I've done this year. I may find time to do another before we leave. It's the light … the light and the sea …. it's what draws me here.'

'Well, the sea is much the same anywhere,' I said. 'Ever

since you learnt to swim, you've always liked the sea – in Australia, New Zealand, France, – all the places you've lived in. There's Brighton, you've always liked Brighton, and it's not far from London.'

'No, no, it's different, it's as if …. oh, I don't know really. I felt the same last year when I first came here. Actually, the first time I came here was with you and I don't remember anything about that. Where did we stay then?'

'Where did we stay?' I said slowly, 'Well, I don't remember, it was a long time ago.'

'But which part? Where was it near?

'Well, it was near the sea,' I said

Krystina burst out laughing. 'Most places are! How did you get there? Where did we stay?'

They were all looking at me, smiling.

'Well, not so far down as here. It was on the other side, I drove through Plymouth. We rented a house, nothing special and quite old, probably pulled down now and replaced with luxury flats. I can't remember the name of the place. We went around a lot, visiting places, it was a long time ago.'

'Didn't you take any photographs?'

'Yes, of course. You will have seen them at the time. But I've no idea what happened to them. Grandma may have had them. The only ones I found after she died were those I sent from Australia.'

'Grandma said we stayed here for a whole month. Sometimes I don't know if I recognize a place or if I'm imagining it.'

My mother had told her, more than once, that soon after my inheritance I had taken her to Cornwall for a holiday and then had gone straight to France and then to Australia. Her words and the tone of incredulity were always the same. 'She was only going for two or three months! And I didn't see you again for five years! You had grown so much! Seven years old! Then there was little James as well! I was so excited when the four of you came back. When I saw you all, I just stood there, staring at you all, speechless.'

I searched for words as I pushed the ice cream around the plate. 'Oh, I don't know. You were only two at the time. It's a known fact that we remember very little of our first five years of life: an isolated image, a scene, an impression, perhaps. We may make assumptions, construct a story around it which, over time, may be far removed from what we actually saw or what we thought we experienced.'

'I remember falling down the stairs,' James interjected. 'And that was on my second birthday at the party. I remember bump, bump, bump, all the way down and my head hurt and there were all these people and you picked me up and carried me into the kitchen.'

'Actually,' I said, 'there were only three people in the hall and your father picked you up while I ran into the kitchen to get some cold water and a tea cloth to put on your head. We don't really remember anything of the first four or five years of our lives, not properly. What I do know, it was an awful fright. I was trembling like a leaf.'

'The details may be wrong but I remember the main part, the important part and I was only just two at the time, so if Krys was two and what, how much?'

'Two and four months …'

'Well, she may remember something.'

'But yours was an accident, James, something quite different and quite a sudden, scary experience, which is why you remember it. Krystina didn't have a scary experience like that. Can you remember anything else about the party?'

'No, probably that was enough,' he laughed.

'Where were you then, Krys?' Anna asked.

'Well, I was obviously there but I remember nothing about it, apart from James talking about it for years.'

'I remember when my grandfather died, I was about three at the time ….' Anna began.

The conversation turned to Anna's memory of her grandfather and we heard no more about real or imagined memories of Cornwall.

The next three days passed quietly. Krystina spent three or four hours each day working before joining us. We went for leisurely walks, stopped for a pub lunch and returned in the late afternoon and talked, then we ate a light supper in the garden. One day, the weather being unsettled, we stayed in, read, cooked and talked about the business and made plans to spend Christmas together in France. It was all very pleasant and easygoing and I began to relax.

She had the painting framed and returned with it wrapped in brown paper. She undid the string around the brown paper, then handed it to James.

'Take this off for me, James,' she said.

Carefully, he undid the sellotape which fastened the folds of paper together.

'Here you are, Krys,' he said with a chuckle.

'When did this bit of irrationality start?' Anna asked. 'What has sellotape ever done to you?'

'I know, it's ridiculous, isn't it?' Krystina said, as puzzled about the reason for this phobia, as Anna was. 'I've never liked it, for as far back as I remember. It sticks to everything and you can't get it off. If I as much as touch it I get really panicky, I feel trapped, I can't breathe.'

'And that can be quite dramatic. She looks as if she's about to faint, then she starts to hyperventilate,' James said.

'People have all sorts of phobias: belts, tape, plasters, glue, they don't like things that may restrict them in some way. It's quite common.' I paused for a few seconds as images from long ago came into my mind, images fixed in time, never to be erased.

When I spoke my words betrayed no emotion; I sounded calm, self-assured. 'She was playing with it one day when she was about six years old and it stuck to her fingers and she thought it wouldn't come off. She tried to bite it off and it stuck to her month. Then she panicked. That seemed to be the cause of it. Don't you remember, Kristina? You were quite hysterical.'

'I'm not sure. You've told me before. We were in New Zealand then.'

'Of course, it's no different from other phobias really. Some people have a fear of flying or falling, of strangers or certain foods. It's not unusual. I knew someone once who had a fear of buttons.'

'Buttons?' Anna exclaimed. 'Why buttons?'

'I don't know. I don't suppose she knew either. We all have our little idiosyncrasies. Without them, we wouldn't be so interesting. Little kinks in our personalities make us what we are. And this painting looks even better now it's been framed.

It's just the right frame for it. It will look wonderful in your office.'

I was adept in moving conversation on and their attention was drawn to the newly framed painting; and, after various expressions of admiration, Krystina placed it on top of a small cupboard where it remained for the rest of the holiday, until yesterday morning when she took it away with her and I left the cottage.

'What will you do when we leave, Mum?' James asked, the night before he and Anna left.

'I shall do what I have been doing so far – read, go for walks, maybe look after the food while Krystina gets on with her article.'

'I won't be working all the time,' Krystina said. 'If I finish the article in good time, I may do some more painting and we'll be going out together. By the way, I'm taking you to the Eden Project on Friday.'

'You'll love it!' Anna exclaimed. 'James and I went there soon after we arrived. It's fascinating. If I lived here I would go three or four times a year, just to see seasonal changes.'

I had heard of the Eden Project, of course, and said I looked forward to going there. Straight up the A30, then across. It would be a pleasant day and would disturb no memories.

James and Anna returned to Sussex. They planned to stay with me for a weekend soon after I returned home. Krystina would return to London after the holiday, her article complete and then she, too, would try to visit me for that weekend so we would all be together again soon.

Sometimes, we stay with Krystina in her two-bedroomed

flat in London. On such weekends we often go to the theatre or an art exhibition and eat out. We are a united family and I love these weekends. I only wished that Krystina could find a really nice man – and there have been some – and settle down, somewhere in the south of England, easy access to London, or even in France where she would still be near to us, her family.

The following Friday, Krystina and I set out early for the Eden Project. We drove up the A30, branching off on to the A390 when we got near Truro and we were there just before it opened. We spent several hours wandering along the meandering paths and the iconic biomes, gazing at thousands of different plants among large crowds who were relaxed and good natured. It was a most lovely day. We left after a late lunch and Krystina insisted on going back a different way.

'It will be more interesting to see something else, something different,' she said, while driving along the A39.

'But it will take much longer, the roads are narrow.'

'But picturesque! We're not in a hurry, we don't have to get back yet. We can stop and have a look around, have a drink or a bite to eat if we get hungry.'

'But where?'

'Well, anywhere! There's Helford, the Lizard, Coverack, Porthleven, Praa Sands, there's dozens of places! Which one? Come on, you choose! There's nothing to hurry back for. Come on, let's make the most of the day.'

I wasn't happy about it but I agreed to take a detour to the Lizard knowing that if we stopped there, we would have no time to stop again on the way back. So, in the late afternoon we walked to the Lizard Point and gazed on the English

Channel and across to Mounts Bay. I cannot spend too long looking at the sea, no matter how tranquil and serene it is on a warm early evening. It threatens me, attempts to draw me in, becomes intensely overwhelming. I shivered.

'Are you cold?'

'A little,' I said, 'the sun has gone down.'

'Come, we'll have a drink and a bite to eat.'

We went to a pub, had a snack and a drink and I said I felt much warmer.

Krystina looked at me intently. 'You do like it here, don't you? It was a good idea coming back this way, wasn't it? We've seen more and it's completed the day.'

I smiled at her. 'It's been a lovely day. Let's not be too late getting back.'

It was gone eight o'clock but still light and warm. The journey back would take a good hour and Krystina drove at a steady pace, commenting on what she saw.

I soon began to recognize that part of Cornwall forever engraved in my memory. The Tregeagle Inn, still dark and forbidding, loomed large as we approached, a mute and threatening reminder of youthful folly.

As Krystina drove past the Tregeagle I wondered what had happened to Mark and where he was now. Could he still be here? The pain of memory was not so acute now, but dull and aching. I wished I had not come here.

Soon after, Krystina branched off onto a minor road, closer to the sea. 'It's prettier,' she said, 'and we can pick up the main road later.'

It was a detour of a few miles but my heart sank as she drove on and I tried to keep my eyes on the road. Ten minutes later an express supermarket and a petrol station caught my attention and I realized they had replaced the little row of shops – all had gone, the general store, the greengrocer's, the bakery, the fish and chip shop. Immediately, I felt the slow, dull thumping of my heart and my eyes were inexorably drawn to the row of small terrace houses ahead.

Pensquidden Terrace was still there, on the right, well maintained, looking brighter, one or two with new attic windows and some with freshly painted, brightly coloured front doors, still, no doubt, let out to holiday-makers. And there, on the end, was number nine, looking just the same, with a white van in front of it, large lettering on the back.

RICHARDS FOR HOUSE EXTENSIONS
Conservatories Kitchens Bathrooms

I thought of the large garden behind the house, unseen from the road, and I wondered if flowers still grew right below the living room window. Tears pricked my eyes and I swallowed hard.

'You're very quiet,' Krystina's voice startled me for a minute. 'Are you tired?'

A terrible sadness overpowered me and I was unable to answer immediately.

She repeated the question, a little louder and I said, 'Oh, I think I was beginning to doze off.'

'We'll be back soon. Then we'll have a nice cup of tea.'

Half an hour later we were drinking tea, reminiscing about the day and, pleading tiredness, I went to bed. I tried consciously to think of other things, to put the past behind me, as I so often had, where it belonged. I took up my book and keeping my voice as low as possible, I began to read aloud in an effort to drive out the thoughts that began to drift into my mind; they withdrew only for seconds before returning, increasingly insistent, wave after wave, with the force of an incoming tide.

It was gone four when, exhausted, I turned off the light. Once more, huge rocks enclose us as we lay on a large white rock, wedged, secluded, in their midst. I feel his arms, lean and muscular around me, holding our almost naked bodies close together; I feel again his hair, his neck, his back and the flat rough stone beneath us, still warm and sparkling in the late afternoon sun. Two people on a sacrificial altar of love.

I cried out as I woke, my heart beating wildly. The dream, which had once haunted my sleep years ago, had returned.

9

Three days later, it was the first item on the Western Evening News, the words announced with the music still fading in the background:

> *The remains of a child have been found in a garden by workmen building a conservatory …..*

I stood up. 'I'm going to make some tea. Do you want a cup?'

'A bit later, let's hear the news first,' Krystina replied, her attention fixed on the television.

'Well, I'll go and get things ready, anyway,' I said and I went in the kitchen, put the kettle on, took out cups and saucers, then sat on the chair with my mind racing all the while. What to do? What to say?

I only went back into the living room when I heard the newsreader talking about some dispute over fishing quotas.

'They've found the remains of a child,' Krystina said, 'buried in a garden. They were extending the living room to make a conservatory.'

'Oh dear,' I said, 'that's sad. I wonder how it came to be buried there.'

'Well, they don't know that yet, of course, or whether it's a boy or a girl, they've only found bones.'

'I expect they'll find it's an animal, someone's pet dog, a large one. They often jump to conclusions, workmen who find bones.'

Krystina looked up at me. 'I expect they're fairly sure if it's announced on the news. They're doing tests.'

'The tea is almost ready. What were they saying about the fishing quotas? Are they arguing about that again? I do think the Cornish have a point. The European Union interferes too much with agriculture and fishing and it affects this part of the country very much. After all, it is their livelihood.'

Krystina looked surprised. 'I didn't know you were so interested in fishing quotas. But you're right. Cornwall is struggling – the tin mining has gone, agriculture and fishing are threatened by competition from outside the county. I just wish more people would buy local produce. A place like this shouldn't just rely on tourism.'

She was off on one of her favourite topics. I had distracted her and I listened and nodded and commented trying to be equally interested and enthusiastic. Later, I suggested that she spent the following day working on her article and perhaps we could go out for the evening – a meal somewhere, a long walk before bed, it would do us good.

I slept little that night. I thought of returning home but I needed to know what was happening. Foolishly, I thought that by staying I had some control over the situation.

The following day went as I had planned, but it was the day after that the situation became more difficult. She had gone out to get milk and bread for breakfast and returned with the paper.

'They think the bones they discovered may be those of a child who went missing thirty years ago. A local child disappeared from the beach and was never found. Some think she must have drowned. Her parents are still living in the area. They've taken the mother's DNA and they'll see if it matches the bones of the child.'

I could not speak. My heart raced and I felt faint. Only when Krystina, registering my silence, turned with a look of concern, did I manage to say, 'It's incredible what they can do with DNA these days.'

'Yes, the police have solved quite a few crimes through DNA, and some were committed years ago. They never really give up on such cases. Every so often an old case is reviewed and these days it's usually DNA that helps them to solve it. It looks very likely that the bones are those of the missing child, about two or three years old, from what they can tell.'

She went on reading the paper. 'It must be awful for the family, not knowing and now everything coming back again. If the DNA tests confirm that it is their child, it will open everything up again, confirm their worst fears. After all they still won't know how their child died, will they?'

I did not answer.

Krystina was not listening. She was engrossed in the paper. 'Listen to this,' she said, 'Mrs. Cynthia Trewin, mother of Merryn Trewin who disappeared thirty years ago, says she never gave up hope that the child would be found alive. Now she and her family may …'

But I could stand it no longer. I left the room and went out into the patch of garden in front of the cottage and sat on the wooden bench. I had to think, think hard, decide what to do. But even as I tried, I knew there was nothing I could do. I would have to wait.

Soon Krystina came hurrying out. 'Mum, what's the matter? You just went! …. Mum, you look awful, you're as pale as a ghost. Do you feel all right?'

'Just a bit faint. It came over me suddenly. I just needed some fresh air. I'll sit here for a while. I'll be all right in a moment.'

'But Mum, has this happened before?'

'It will go in a minute. Don't look so worried, Krystina, it's nothing much, just tiredness, that's all, and too much bad news in the world.'

'Well, sit down and rest for a while. I'll make you a cup of tea.'

That ended the conversation about the missing child for a while and after I drank the tea I sat quietly in the chair, pretending to read.

In the late afternoon I suggested we went for a walk. 'We can eat out, find a nice little pub somewhere.'

'Let's do that tomorrow. We can go out for the whole day, I know a good place for lunch. I've got some work to finish tonight and we've got food in the fridge. We can go for a stroll later, after eating.'

So, again, we watched the evening news. I didn't want to, but Krystina was watching and so I had to know. It began with an interview with Cynthia Trewin.

I did not feel as I did when I saw her on a small black and white television all those years ago. Then, I had felt only dislike and contempt for this woman who was blubbering on television about how she had only left her children on the beach for a few minutes, how she had told Merryn not to go in the water, how she didn't believe she had drowned, please could everyone look for her, please, please find her.

The facts were clear. Cynthia Trewin had left her daughter, nearly three years old, alone on the beach with her six year old brother and she had left them, not for a few minutes, but for half an hour while she went to get them some chips for their afternoon tea on the beach. Two children, a six year old and a two year old! Half an hour! A lot can happen in half an hour. It was an error of judgement, and in that she was no better than the rest of us. She had only herself to blame. I had felt no pity for her.

Now, as I watched the interview, I saw an older version of her former self, a woman who spoke calmly and with simple dignity of coming to terms with loss, yet never completely losing hope that her child was still alive .

I realized how much I had hardened my heart against her in those few minutes thirty years ago and how I had not given her a single thought since then. I couldn't help feeling a stirring of pity for her, but I told myself it was all in the past now. We all have to come to terms with tragedy, there comes a time when you have to move on.

It was with a growing sense of dismay that I noticed that Krystina was riveted. She looked at the television with the same intensity she gave at times to her research papers. She muttered a few words, now and then throughout the interview. 'Awful … not knowing …. she seems a nice woman, doesn't she?'

It was at this point that she looked up at me and I was compelled to answer.

'Probably.'

The interview, no more than two minutes, but two long minutes of anguish for me, finished at last and another began with the police officer in charge of the investigation. Painful though this was, it must at least be more endurable than listening to Cynthia Trewin, I thought. I listened with acute attention to the information that followed, such as it was at this stage of the investigation. During this time the camera zoomed in on the site where the bones had been found. There was a close shot of the white tent, two white-clothed forensic scientists nearby, before the camera surveyed the scene from over the back fence of the garden with the large tree close to the back gate.

Krystina gave a start. She looked at me with amazement. 'I've seen it before! I've been there!'

I could not speak for a moment and she took my silence for incomprehension.

'There! There! The tree in the garden!' She pointed to the television screen. 'I've been there! I ran to it. Or round it. I can't remember. I was frightened! Really scared! Someone was chasing me!'

'But Krystina, what are you talking about? You haven't been anywhere near there in the last couple of weeks, have you?'

'No, no, not now! A long time ago. I was scared. Someone was after me. I remember!'

'Perhaps you saw something when we passed by the other day,' I said, 'and you can't quite place the memory. A sort of deja vu feeling.'

'Did we pass by there? Yes, it must be somewhere near there. Did you notice that? You were dozing off.'

'Oh, I didn't see anything. I don't know where it is.'

We watched the rest of the news but I could tell her thoughts were wandering, her concentration was gone. The tree. The chase. The fear. It was all playing on her mind.

'I wonder how they have managed over the years?' she said, as if not really expecting an answer.

So I did not answer.

'I mean, it's something you can never forget, isn't it? Always there, at the back of your mind. It's awful.'

'Yes,' I said, 'it is. If you keep dwelling on things that happened years ago, it can destroy your life. Do you want some more wine?'

She didn't answer but held out her glass and I filled it with a rather good Bordeaux. 'Do you know,' I said, 'that this was very popular in this country some nine hundred years ago? Eleanor of Aquitaine brought it in.'

'I had no idea this bottle was that old,' she said and we both laughed. The conversation then moved on to wine.

We watched television after dinner, a documentary about penguins and I forced myself to make the occasional comment. 'Oh, look at that … isn't that extraordinary?' She murmured something unintelligible in reply and I knew she was not really listening. Every now and then she gazed thoughtfully at the floor, then she sat back and stared at the television; sometimes her lips moved a little, soundlessly, the slight frown on that high smooth forehead exposing some inner agitation.

Yet when the programme ended, she got up decisively from her chair. 'Come on, she said, 'a walk before bedtime. It will do us good.'

So we walked and talked about the number of visitors who were still out strolling through the narrow streets and listened to the sound of the night waves as they rhythmically, gratingly, drew back on the sea shore. When we returned she made two mugs of hot chocolate.

'Here you are, just what we need for a good night's sleep.'

We went to bed but the drink did not help. I slept fitfully, only half consciously; so, as soon as I felt the hard stone beneath me, his lips on mine, I was able to struggle, desperately pulling myself up out of the dream until I found myself, eyes wide open, sitting up in bed, my heart beating, my hands trembling.

Krystina did not sleep well either, for I heard her turning throughout the night. I heard her get up and open the window, turn on the light, and she must have read for a while before trying to sleep again. It was half past six when I heard her get up again, go to the bathroom, then into the kitchen. I heard the gentle click of the door and knew she was trying not to wake me. I thought perhaps she had gone to get milk, but then I heard the engine of the car and, as I reached the window, I saw it turning out of the driveway and into the road and watched until it disappeared from sight.

10

It was gone nine when she returned. I heard the car and set about making the tea. She walked straight into the kitchen and said, 'I've been there! I know I have!'

'What on earth are you talking about? Been where?' I did not look at her, my voice was light but I could not disguise the slight quaver.

'Pensquidden Lane.'

I felt as if I had been suddenly winded by a terrible blow.

'What? You've been all the way over there this morning? Whatever for?'

'I had to see the place. I don't remember the front of the house or the road. But I stood at the back, looked over the wall and I knew, just as I did when they showed it on television. It's the tree. I was trying to hide. I was very, very frightened.'

'That's very strange. Perhaps ...'

'Mum, you must remember something. Did I go there? Did you know other people with young children when you took me to Cornwall all those years ago? Perhaps I had been invited round to play with another child at that house. It would help if you could remember where we stayed.'

'Well, I don't. I thought it was further up the coast, somewhere nearer to Falmouth.' My mind was racing, trying to think of explanations. Nothing. There was nothing.

'Falmouth is several miles away from Pensquidden Lane, isn't it?' There was no mistaking the disbelief in her voice. 'Did someone else look after me sometimes? Could they have taken me there?'

'No, you were with me all the time.'

'But I was there, in that garden. And someone was chasing me. Perhaps I saw something then. Something odd. That's why I was frightened. I could have been with other children, that child, perhaps … there must be an explanation.'

'Krystina, this is ridiculous! You were not there. There's no explanation.'

'But it was the same time that the little girl disappeared, the same year, the same month.' She spoke emphatically, indicating there was no point in denying it. Then her tone changed, she spoke slowly, pensively, 'There was something … something I didn't understand and somebody was chasing me … Mum, you *must* remember something, you *must!*' Her voice, though low, was urgent, almost desperate.

'I think you're letting your imagination run away with you.'

'Try to remember! Where did we go? What did we do? Who did you meet? Somebody must know something!'

'Perhaps you should ask the owner of the house. That would be the most logical thing to do,' I said, slightly dismissively.

'The present owner only bought the house a few weeks ago. It has changed hands three times in the last thirty years. The owner back then owned four houses in Pensquidden Lane, he lived in one and used the other three for renting. He sold them six years ago when he went in a home. He's still alive, nearly ninety now. They're questioning him. These are the facts up to now. Do you think he will still have records of all the holiday lets he's ever had? I suppose it's unlikely after thirty years but the police said …'

'What police? How do you know all this?'

'Oh, I was chatting to one of the policemen there on duty this morning. They saw me looking over the garden wall and one came up to say I couldn't stay there so I told him I came to see the place because I thought I recognized it on the television. I said I'm sure I remembered the tree and running away or trying to hide, something like that.'

'I'm surprised he gave you that information about the house. Usually, they don't discuss … '

'Oh, it was nothing more than you can read in the newspaper. Look, I bought one on the way home.'

She took a newspaper out of her shopping bag and gave it to me and I put it on the table without looking.

'He did say that if I really was there all those years ago and remembered anything else, to let them know, any information could be helpful in a murder enquiry.'

'Murder! How do they know?'

'Well, it's obvious really, isn't it? It can't really be anything else, can it? A missing child, bones buried in the garden.'

'Did he take your name and address?'

'No, of course not. He was very nice, quite chatty, just saying the obvious and probably didn't take me very seriously; after all I was only two at the time.'

'Exactly. Two year olds indulge in fantasy. They make things up..'

'But, I *know* I was there! I know, as I know that I'm standing here now. I couldn't sleep last night. That tree in the garden! I couldn't get it out of my mind! I need to find out the dates, who was living there at the time. There'll be some records somewhere, a visitors' letting book, cheque payments, perhaps. How long do banks keep them? There's bound to be an appeal for people living around there at the time or staying there on holiday, to come forward. Someone may remember something.'

I thought of Mr. and Mrs. Goodman, from Scotland. They may remember us. They'd be very old now, nearly eighty perhaps. There was the woman in the flowered dress with twins, although I doubt if she would remember.

'Sooner or later even you will remember. I can't believe you don't remember where we stayed. Your prodigious memory of past events doesn't usually allow you to suffer from amnesia.'

There was an unusual note of scepticism, perhaps mockery, in her voice as she looked at me intently, watching for my reaction.

I knew then I would not be able to prevaricate for much longer. It was all getting too close: the police, Cynthia Trewin, the missing child. Krystina would not rest until that niggling memory made some sort of sense in her mind.

'You would have been in Cornwall more or less at the same time that the little girl went missing. It was September. Surely, you would have heard something about it, it was on the news, there was a big search.' She paused, clearly expecting me to say something, and when I didn't she said softly, 'You've been oddly reticent about the time we spent here, that same September. It's not like you.'

Still I said nothing. My legs felt weak and I sat down on the chair by the kitchen table.

'Mum, you're keeping something from me. What is it? What's wrong?'

There was no way out. I could prevaricate no longer. 'Krystina,' I said, 'sit down a minute.' I took a few sips of tea before I began. My mouth was dry and the words came out slowly, with a slight tremor. 'Of course, I remember. We did stay in that house.'

'We *did?*' Her voice rose in disbelief, her eyes widened in shock. She was silent for a few seconds, staring at me. 'But why didn't you say?'

'It was an awful time. I wanted to protect you.'

'Protect me? From what?'

'From what had happened.'

'But I'm not two years old! I'm thirty two!'

'No, no, I mean *then.*'

I paused, disconcerted, knowing I had to tell her something, something credible, close to the truth, while keeping the essential truth from her. That she must never know. I was not sure what to say next, how much to say, how to say it. She was not just curious about the case, she already felt some emotional involvement with it. She needed answers and I knew she would search for them until she found them.

'You see,' I continued, 'we were not far from where the little girl was lost. At first, everyone, quite sensibly, assumed she had been drowned, as that is obviously what happened. The lifeboat went out, the helicopter searched the bay. They found nothing, although that doesn't mean anything. Every year, people drown in Cornwall, sometimes the bodies are never found. It wasn't until the following day, that they thought she *may* have been abducted, although if that had been the case she would have been taken well out of Cornwall by then. Nevertheless, there was a huge hunt for her. People checked garages, cellars, cupboards in case she had wandered off or had been hidden there. The landlord called and checked the garden and every room of that house while we were there. 'Just in case, you never know,' he said. It was past nine o'clock at night and you were fast asleep. Evans was his name, he may even remember us, given the circumstances.'

'But why didn't you tell me? Why pretend you didn't know?'

I drank some more tea, breathed deeply. 'Krystina, I was so worried about you and I saw danger everywhere. So did everyone else at that time. If someone had abducted a child from a beach, then all children were at risk. People guarded their children like hawks. And so I guarded you. I would not take you to the beach anymore. You were not allowed to leave my side, even when playing in the garden. I was quite paranoid about it. You must understand that I'd never really had complete responsibility for you until that holiday. Grandma had looked after you much of the time and I was far too anxious and full of apprehension.'

'But it's natural for people to be worried in these circumstances. It's a normal reaction. People don't hide it for years.'

'My reactions at the time were extreme, irrational. In fact, I think I was a bit unhinged.'

She gave a little laugh. 'You are one of the sanest people I know.'

'But I wasn't *then*. The responsibility of looking after you all on my own, the disappearance of the child, whatever the reason for it, and my obsession with the constant proximity of death, preyed on my mind. I was too strict, too severe with you and you could not possibly understand. You reacted, of course, any child would. There were screaming tantrums, tears, long silences.'

Inwardly, I was in turmoil, but I spoke with a degree of confidence which I hoped would beguile her into believing me. 'You were very difficult then and I made it worse by being too protective. Not just then, after that …. *incident* … in Cornwall, but all the time we were in France. I wouldn't let you out of my sight.'

'But I remember being frightened … and running … the tree … what … who was I running away from?'

'Me.'

I poured more tea, which, in spite of the self control I exerted over my voice, slopped on to the saucer. 'You were running away from me, screaming your little head off. You wanted to go out to the beach but I wouldn't let you. You were tired of staying in the house and the garden day after day, and the weather was hot. I said you couldn't go out and you ran towards the back gate. For a moment I thought you would run out and I panicked. I shouted at you, very loudly, and ran after you. And I picked you up, just by the tree, and took you in the house. I think I was quite as hysterical as you were. It took me quite a while to calm you down.'

I paused as I remembered the way I had silenced her, what I had done, the effect it had. I was so afraid that the memory would come flooding back to her. How much she remembered and what she was thinking during this silence I do not know.

'It was not your fault, of course. I knew that. Later that night, when you were finally fast asleep, I knew I had reacted unreasonably. It was psychologically damaging.'

Krystina laughed, my words had amused her. 'Now you're exaggerating! And you're sitting there looking so worried! Mum, it was a long time ago! I'm sure you reacted quite normally under the circumstances and you're the last person to psychologically damage anyone.'

'I didn't handle it well," I said seriously. 'I told you off, said it wasn't safe to go out, it frightened you. Then I felt guilty. I couldn't wait to get away, far away, to a safer place.'

'But you didn't go home. We went to France, didn't we?'

'Yes, I had planned to do that, in time for the grape picking.'

'So, was it better there?'

'Of course, although you wanted your grandmother all the time. You talked about her constantly.'

'But why didn't you tell me all this before?'

'I wanted to forget it, never to be reminded of it. Hysterical mothers who are paranoid about safety and death are not good for children. Sometimes I think it did have an effect on you, made you less secure, more ....'

Krstina laughed. 'Now, whose imagination is running away with her? I don't have any problems, not real problems, do I? You, Dad, James, we were a pretty normal family and quite a privileged one. When family life is as secure as ours, children get over minor traumas, they're part of childhood.'

This is exactly what I had told myself a hundred times over the years. Hearing her say it made me feel much better, as if it made up for the lies I was telling her.

'Yes, I suppose they are. Anyway, I couldn't wait to get

away from the place and forget about it. I couldn't explain this to you, you were too young to understand. Some things are best left unsaid and forgotten.'

Krystina was quiet for a while. Then, 'But I don't know why you couldn't have said this earlier this week.' Her voice became increasingly agitated, 'Not remembering where we stayed … not mentioning any of this before … not even when it was on the news … I can't understand why … '

I cut in quickly, firmly, 'Krystina, it was a horrible experience! I pushed it to the back of my mind – and yours, too. That may have been wrong, but I felt it was important for you then, all those years ago, I wanted the memory obliterated, never to be revived. That is how I felt and still feel. I hate thinking about it. Do you understand?'

'Well, yes, I suppose I do. It's a bit extreme but if you were in an extreme state then, perhaps it's only natural that the recollection would be upsetting.' She seemed to be trying to understand but did not sound convinced.

A few seconds passed before I spoke. 'Yes, I was in an extreme state – and so were you. I'm sorry it has all come to light now. I don't want even the memory to spoil this holiday.'

'It won't,' she said. 'Now that it's all out in the open, we'll get on with the rest of the holiday.'

We said little as we prepared a late breakfast and then sat down to eat while listening to music on the radio. I went over our conversation in my head, checking small details, my mind flitting from one room to another in Nine Pensquidden Terrace, the garden, the tree. I made occasional comments about the music, the weather, and hoped she would not notice that I was unable to swallow the food in front of me.

Krystina responded to my comments while she ate. Then: 'But the bones! The bones were buried there. Why there? That is what I can't understand.'

'I can't either. Perhaps they were already there.'

'But if they are the bones of the little girl …'

'We don't know that yet. If they are, then obviously they were buried there much later.'

'Yes, I suppose so.'

She was quiet for a few moments. Then, 'But aren't you curious to know how they came to be there? I am. I mean when you have lived in a place … when something happens, even before or after, there's a feeling that … well, you're bound to be curious. You can't be totally indifferent about it. It's natural to want to know more.'

She had no idea of the anguish she was causing me and the effort it took to dissemble.

'Prying, I would call it, snooping around in things that don't concern us.'

'That's a bit harsh. After all, in a somewhat tenuous way, we are connected to the case, as many other people will be. You said yourself how much it had affected you. So, in a peculiar, remote way, there is a connection, isn't there?'

'Only vicariously and I don't think that's very healthy. We are not really connected to it, not then, not now. As far as I'm concerned, it was an unpleasant memory and best forgotten.'

'Even so, I'd like to know more about it. I may go into the newspaper office and look at past papers – they may be on-line in the library– the *Western Morning News* or *The Cornishman* will have reported it at the time, there was a big search for her, there'll be interviews with all sorts of people.'

'Everything that was known then will be in the local papers you have already read this week. There's been enough of it on the television. Now stop this useless morbid attraction. You are getting obsessive about it. It is quite unwholesome.'

It was the best I could do. It sounded plausible. She said no more about it for the rest of the day and only occasionally did I catch her looking pensively out of the window towards the sea.

Krystina had almost finished her article and I was glad when she began to focus her mind on editing it. I tried to read a book but could not concentrate. I made an early evening meal – a favourite French dish, and opened a bottle of Sancerre, another favourite. Afterwards we went for a walk. She was in good spirits, the article was finished, ready for printing and posting. She made various suggestions about how we should spend the rest of the week and I suggested a trip to the Scilly Isles, so we agreed to sleep on it and decide in the morning.

I slept fitfully and got up early and prepared breakfast. It was ready by the time Krystina arrived at the table and we ate and chatted in a pleasant, relaxed atmosphere. We talked about the vineyard in France, the grape picking which would start at the end of the month. We talked of the times we went there with Jeff, soon after we had returned from New Zealand. Krystina said she remembered the first time she went there when she was about eight and how much she wanted to speak French.

'I was so excited about everything there, it was so different! The Loire Valley, the vines, the chateau! I'd never lived in anything like the chateau before. Of course, I had gone there with you, when I was younger, before we went to Australia, but I don't remember anything about it.'

'Of course you wouldn't, you were far too young.'

'What exactly did we do on that holiday?'

'Well, Uncle Martin … '

'No, before then, when we were here, in Cornwall. It must have been a bit of a trial for you with a two year old in tow.'

The subject had returned again. She couldn't keep away from it for long. I answered in a slow, detached way, betraying none of the anxiety I felt inside.

'No, not at the beginning. We travelled around a lot. I took you to see so many places, basically because *I* wanted to see them. You were mainly interested in the beach, the tourist attractions which had play areas for children and ice cream. In France, you seemed to be overwhelmed by people speaking a language you didn't understand and you became quite subdued. You felt much more at home in Australia.'

'You would have liked to stay there, or in New Zealand, wouldn't you?'

'At the time, yes. It was the novelty factor. Everything seemed more exciting. But it wasn't very practical. My business was here. And Jeff, of course, was under a timed contract there, so there was no question of staying.'

'Did you ever regret it?'

'Regret what?'

'Well, going off like that. Making sudden decisions. Grandma said …..'

'Oh, no, no, of course not. I was young, I had money. It

was all an adventure. A bit impulsive, that's all. It was lovely being with you all the time. It made up for the time when Grandma and Diane spent more time with you than I did. And I really think all that travelling was good for you, seeing all those places, meeting lots of different people, eating different types of food. It was an education in itself. It did you the world of good. Just the two of us. I loved it. Then I met Jeff and then I had James. I have been very lucky. There has never been anything to regret.'

There has never been anything to regret. My voice, I know, was bright and decisive as I said these words. She would never know how hollow they were, how saying them made me feel sick. For years I had regretted everything. For years I wished Grandmere had left every franc to Uncle Martin. I had longed to be still working at Nichols and Wilson. My whole being ached to go home each night to my mother and Diane and Krystina. It was ordinary life, real honest life; I ate well and slept well. I was safe. I was free.

Those last few days in Cornwall had been a nightmare. Driving around Cornwall with a difficult, fractious, two year old was a frightening ordeal and my nerves were fraught with worry and fear. I would leave the house early in the morning, and drive far away from Pensquidden Terrace. We went to Newquay, to Padstow, to Tintagel and as far as Bude and Plymouth. Returning late, I would park the car in the makeshift garage at the back of the house. I wanted no one to see us; and, as much as I longed for Mark and to run into his arms, I knew, no matter what he, too, may be suffering, I must never see him again.

However tired I felt, sleep did not take pity on me, and I spent much of the night tormented by thoughts until, in a futile effort to forget or travel back in time, I would hide beneath the bedclothes, hugging the pillow, whispering his name, fleetingly clinging to another memory; and in such a state of escapism I sought comfort and forgetfulness, however transitory. I could not wait for the week to end, to hand back the keys of 9 Pensquidden Terrace, and drive out of Cornwall forever and sail to France to begin my long and painful exile.

By the time I returned, my five year sentence of slow and acutely painful time was coming to an end and hope began to creep into the grief and constant fear that had consumed me. Such is the healing power of time and the resilience of the human spirit, that I could not help but think that I was indeed fortunate. I had come through my darkest hours and the years that followed were kind to me.

I had two children who needed and loved me. James is as perfect a son as anyone could wish to have, as good-natured as he is good-looking, hard working, easy-going, a bit of an extrovert. Krystina is serious-minded, independent, thoughtful, a little introverted, but she is often lively and amusing, and she is helpful, always sensitive to the needs of others. She is my achievement in life, no mother has cared for or loved a child more than I have cared for and loved her.

'What are you thinking?' Krystina's voice interrupted my reverie. 'You were far away then.' Her eyes gazed into mine, as if trying to read my thoughts.

'I was thinking,' I replied slowly as though weighing up some weighty problem in my mind, 'I was thinking we could go back to Australia or New Zealand next year for a holiday. Would you like that?'

'Possibly, although I had thought of coming back here.'

'You may remember some of the places you saw there. Those countries have memories for you, too.'

'Yes, I do remember some things: the school, the grapes. Then Dad and James.'

'You were very happy there.'

'I've been happy here – and in France.'

'Yes, I suppose you have.'

She looked at me attentively. 'But you're not so sure. You don't worry about me, do you? I mean, whether I've been happy or not?'

'No, no, of course not. Well, no more than most parents, I expect. When you were small, Grandma was always saying what a happy little soul you were.'

'The last time I saw Grandma she seemed to be living completely in the past. She thought I was still two years old.'

'She wasn't remembering anything coherently at the end. I don't think she recognized James the last time he went to see her and once she asked me who I was.'

'I wonder why people, as they get older, remember the past more than the present? Were they happier then? Or are they escaping from the present? Which is better, when you are old – to live in the past or the present? I mean there's not much point in living for the future, is there?'

'I think they remember the past because the present is so limited for them, it offers so little. It's different for others; too many, without the excuse of age, dwell on the past, letting it dominate their lives. It's a form of escapism, and quite unhealthy."

'But we have spent a lot of time reminiscing this week.

115

We've been to France, New Zealand, Australia and back. You wouldn't want to forget about that, would you?'

'No, of course not. Those are good memories worth remembering. They have a positive effect.'

'But they make our present, they shape what we see and feel in the present.'

'Of course, I didn't mean that they were always best forgotten.'

'But even what is forgotten also shapes the way we are now. In living in the present we can't help but have the past with us. In many ways, we are what the past has made us.'

'We can always start afresh and shape our present according to the way we want it. It's called free will.'

'So a decision made today about tomorrow can be made irrespective of the past and as a result of free will?'

I replied hesitantly, 'More or less,' but I knew I had fallen into a trap.

'But today will be tomorrow's past and so tomorrow's present will be shaped by the past.'

I laughed. 'You are being too metaphysical. I should have seen that coming.'

She smiled but continued in more serious vein: 'But the past, both what we remember and what we forget, shapes our present and we take that and all we accumulate in the present, every minute, every day, into the future. Unless we acknowledge that and attempt to understand it, we won't really understand ourselves, who we are, where we are coming from, where we are going.'

'That's true, up to a point. I just feel it's dangerous to rely too much on the past. We all have different memories and interpretations of it. Sometimes, looking back, one sees the past differently from the way it happened at the time. We don't always remember things as they were and we choose what we want to remember. It can be very misleading.'

'You mean we re-invent the past?'

'Most people do. It's part of human nature. It satisfies their present needs or perceptions.'

'Perhaps it helps to keep them sane.' She paused, thought for a moment and said, 'But if they re-invent the past, their present is actually based on a lie, a distortion of the truth.'

'I expect that's true of many people, perhaps most.'

'But they are in thrall to a lie, a misrepresentation of their own making.'

'Yes, either consciously or subconsciously.'

'Subconsciously is damaging, consciously is reprehensible.'

I recognised that distinctive critical tone she often used when discussing some issues to do with her work. It would appear in a lecture or an article as a not too thinly veiled criticism of something, often some legal nicety or some aspect of government policy.

'It must have a detrimental effect on them. It holds them back, hiding behind a fabrication,' she continued.

'Facing facts is sometimes too difficult,' I countered.

She was silent for a few moments. 'It may be difficult, but in the long run, it must be better. Otherwise people fool themselves, they don't understand themselves, don't know who they really are, they screw up their lives, and often the lives of other people.' She paused briefly, before continuing: 'Religion gets it right sometimes, once you get behind all the paraphernalia that goes with it. You find your own enlightenment, meditate for it, no one can do it for you. What about, "Seek, and you shall find" and "The truth will set you free"?' She paused again. 'It's true, though, isn't it? I mean, from both a psychological and moral point of view.'

'Perhaps, but all I'm really saying is that we must look back with caution, learn from that which is beneficial and positive. We must be selective in what we search for. Too many choose to live in the past instead of getting on with things in the here and now. Obsessive mental digging is morbid and destructive. Some things are best ….'

'Buried and forgotten,' she finished the sentence for me.

'Exactly.'

I sat wordless for several seconds, trying to calm my thoughts. If Krystina noticed, she said nothing but moved towards the window.

'I have to go into Penzance,' she said, 'I'm going to the library to do some photocopying, Then I'll post my article. I'll also find out what time the boat sails to the Scilly Isles. You've never been to the islands, have you?'

'No.'

'Then it will be a new experience; hopefully, a positive one.' She looked at the clock. 'I'd better be going, it's almost ten o'clock. Do you want to come with me?'

I did not want to go into Penzance and the conversation had made me anxious. I needed to be on my own for a while.

'No, I think I'll have a rest and finish my book before going for a nice, long walk this afternoon. I need to blow the cobwebs away.'

'Good idea. I should be back some time in the afternoon.'

She cleared the table, then gathered her things together,

put her laptop in its case, carried everything to the car and, within half an hour, followed by a cheerful, 'See you later,' she was gone.

★

I sat brooding for a while, but there was only a week to go and we would be busy doing things, seeing places, together. Then we would be far away from this place.

I spent the next hour or so with my book, restless and only half escaping into fiction. I had a long, hot shower, dressed, drank more tea. I wished that I had gone with her. I wanted her to return soon. I found myself worrying about traffic and accidents. I came close to believing I was having a premonition, something bad was about to happen. I told myself it was nothing more than the morning's conversation that had unsettled me. I needed to pull myself together.

It was gone one o'clock when I stepped out of the cottage into a fresh breeze blowing across the sea, but I turned away from the sea and went up into narrow lanes that threaded their way through scattered houses, then fields, past small farms and on to the moors thick with bracken and gorse. White clouds cheerfully dotted a blue sky and the light from sun and sea permeated that landscape which had remained wild and untamed for centuries.

I must have walked for a good five miles and the walk had done me good. It had blown away those irrational fears which had tormented me since I had arrived here. I felt somewhat transformed; my mood was lighter, I was at ease with myself. As I made my way back in the late afternoon I began to look forward to the evening ahead.

I returned by a different route, so that I approached the cottage from the back. I let myself in through the back door and realized straight away that Krystina had returned and was talking to someone in the living room. We had spoken to one or two of the neighbours since we had been here but we had never had visitors. I listened, not making out actual words but hearing only the murmur of two voices, both talking intently, effortlessly, as if they already knew each other. I wondered for a moment if she had met a friend or colleague who was also on holiday and I was idly browsing through a list of her friends in my mind as I opened the living room door.

Her visitor was in the process of putting her cup of tea on the coffee table as Krystina said, 'Ah, Mum, you're back.'

At that point, her visitor, sitting in the chair opposite her, looked up at me and I found myself face to face with Cynthia Trewin.

11

My legs buckled beneath me and I fell, knocking into the armchair which prevented me from falling to the floor.

'Mum!' Krystina jumped up from her chair and ran over to me, helping me up into the armchair. 'What happened? Are you all right?'

'I ….. I … just felt a bit faint. It's nothing, just …' my voice seemed far away, I struggled to speak.

Worried, she looked at me closely. 'Where have you been? What happened?'

'Nothing. It's nothing.'

A voice cut in. 'Stand back a bit, dear, I'll put your mother's feet up on this stool.'

They lifted my feet on the stool and Krystina dutifully filled a cup with tea and brought it to me. I took it, the cup shaking in the saucer so badly I had to hold both separately.

'Mum, where did you go? How far did you walk?'

'I'm not sure … it was such a nice day … about ten miles, perhaps.'

'Your mother probably overdid the walking and it's been very warm today.'

Cynthia Trewin's voice – the pace, the intonation, the slight accent, – although softly spoken sounded very, very close, her words penetrated into my brain.

'That's too far to go on your own. You should have waited for me. I haven't been back long.' Krystina looked at her visitor, then back at me. 'Mum, this is Mrs Trewin. We met in the newspaper office.'

'I'm pleased to meet you, Mrs. Bentley.'

My heart was thudding and there was a tightness in my chest as I looked at a woman, not far off sixty, standing right in front of me, wearing a navy blue dress with a loose white jacket and dark sandals. Her dark hair was lightly streaked with grey and fell in a thick, natural wave to her neck. I could think of nothing to say, but it was not necessary as Krystina turned her attention to me.

'You must see the doctor, Mum, as soon as you get back. This isn't like you.'

'It's probably nothing to worry about, but it would be sensible to go for a check-up,' Cynthia Trewin said, supporting Krystina's words. Then she returned to her chair and sipped some more tea.

Krystina pulled her chair a little closer and every so often glanced solicitously at me while talking to Cynthia Trewin, both including me in their conversation although thoughtfully requiring no contribution from me. They talked mainly about various walks in the area, the footpath routes across country, the coastal path, and the need for care and vigilance in hot weather and during winter gales.

Over the next half an hour – and this is the only time I met her – I began to notice more about her, things I recognized. She had a thoughtful, slightly penetrating gaze when listening, she spoke in a calm, measured tone. She was considerate and levelheaded without pretension or self-pity. Someone who, in normal circumstances, I would have liked.

I had seen her twice on television, the focus of attention; for years I had effectively erased her from my memory. Now she was stealing back and here, in this room, close, too close to me, she appeared remarkably ordinary and chillingly significant.

Soon, she looked at her watch, put her cup on the table and picked up her handbag. 'Well, I'll be on my way. You have the evening ahead of you.'

'You don't have to rush away and I'll give you a lift to your sister's.'

'Oh, no, I wouldn't hear of it! It's not very far and you need to be with your mother.'

They both looked at me kindly. I could not bear it, but could think of nothing to say to divert their attention. Krystina broke the silence which may have only lasted for seconds: 'How are you feeling now, Mum?'

'Oh, much better. I don't know what came over me,' I said, my heart still beating fast, but I sat up straighter, in an effort to convince them and also to prepare myself for the inevitable goodbyes which would follow. I could not wait for her to leave.

Krystina had other ideas, for she topped up my cup with more tea and poured another cup for her visitor who thanked her, put her bag on the floor and settled back into her chair. This would keep her there for another half an hour and I dreaded each moment.

Somehow, this changed the tenor of the conversation. Both Krystina and Cynthia Trewin seemed more relaxed, perhaps as they were before I had intruded so dramatically into the room. We sipped our tea in silence but not for long. I had scarcely spoken since I came in and wished only to stay in my chair and say nothing. But Cynthia Trewin, no doubt out of politeness, tried to draw me into the conversation. Also, she may have been hoping for more information, although I could not tell her more than Krystina would already have told her.

'Krystina tells me you stayed in Pensquidden Terrace that summer.'

'Yes, for four weeks. We didn't use the house much, just to sleep in. We went around a lot ...' My voice did not sound like my own, it seemed far away, as if I were coming out of an anaesthetic.

'You don't remember seeing or hearing anything unusual about the garden.' The tone implied a question.

'No, I'm afraid I don't.'

'Of course, you would have been on the beach; it's just a few minutes from the house.'

'We went a couple of times, we travelled around a lot. Krystina didn't like the water much in those days.'

'Merryn loved the water. We used to call her the water baby. She loved going to that beach ... Of course, we don't know yet if it is Merryn. I've always thought ...' She spread her hands out a little, an empty gesture, like someone who has nothing to hold on to.

'This must be a very difficult time for you,' Krystina said.

Cynthia Trewin's tone of voice changed, at once more fluent and self-possessed, as if she had responded to this remark many times before.

'We have always known that Merryn may be dead, even from the beginning, but while there was a possibility that she may still be alive, then you hope that is the case. There were a couple of supposed sightings of her at the beginning but they turned out to be false. It's different this time because they have actually found a body and it may be… it's possible….' She faltered a moment, unable to finish and for a few seconds we sat in silence.

In a voice almost reduced to a whisper, she said, 'I am hoping it is not her. I cannot bear to think what may have happened to her, how she came to be buried there. I really hope it is not her.' She looked at us, worried, troubled. 'And that is an awful thing to think, isn't it? In hoping it isn't her, I must be wishing that it's someone else's child.'

Her words, sharp as needles, pierced through me. I was silent. There was nothing I could say.

She paused before resuming, a little more briskly, 'We don't know yet. The police said we must not jump to conclusions, it is by no means certain. So until we get the DNA results, we have to keep an open mind.'

'Well, where there's any uncertainty, it's only natural to hope,' Krystina spoke softly, sympathetically.

'Oh, we have hoped for years! When you don't know what has happened, you imagine all sorts of possibilities and some are so horrific that you take refuge in kinder thoughts, – she was safe, nearby, perhaps, and then you imagine that you can find her.'

She paused in thought for a moment and then continued in a lower, more confidential tone, 'Very few people know this, – and I'm not quite sure why I'm telling you now, – but in the early days I even hoped to find her myself. I looked at every child I saw in the street, I'd follow any who vaguely resembled her, and it's surprising how many did – or I thought they did. I trailed the streets for miles around here, all the beaches, looking, just looking.'

Krystina was clearly imagining the scene as I was myself and the pointless futility of it. She was captivated, whereas I wanted to flee from that room and hear no more. Had I been able to I would have done so, but my heart was pounding in a body that was too weak to move.

'After her fifth birthday I would sometimes find myself looking through the railings into school playgrounds. I couldn't pass a school without looking. I looked for her among a hundred children as they played during the morning break or as they left the school and joined their waiting parents. I knew that was an absurd thing to do, she couldn't possibly have been there. Bill said I must stop doing it, it would drive me mad. But he, too, couldn't walk down a street without glancing at every child he saw.

It did get better, of course; you can't go on living that way. Time moves on. But you never really give up. In some ways we never stopped looking. We are more realistic now, now so many years have passed. I know it's very unlikely that we shall ever find her; but unless we have real, concrete evidence that she is no longer alive, we can't help hoping, can we?'

'I suppose after the initial search is over, people stop looking and you are left on your own,' Krystina said.

'Yes, people are very good when they think they can help, but as time passes they realize there is nothing more that they can do and they have their own lives to lead. Eventually, it's what

126

we had to try to do ourselves though it was difficult. I know some still believe that she drowned and I can understand why they think so, but I've never believed it myself. It seems so unlikely. My sister is sure she was abducted. She organized a public prayer vigil for Merryn thinking that would somehow help. She still goes to church every Sunday evening and prays for Merryn's return.'

I managed to speak, to show an interest. 'Do you find that helpful?' I said as neutrally as possible.

'In the early days, a lot of people prayed for Merryn's return. I did too, although I don't have a strong belief in anything like that. On the other hand, I suppose it does no harm and it makes my sister feel as if she's doing something. I understand that. Sometimes when all fails, there's nothing else left.'

'Yes, I understand that,' I said and did not add what I thought: *You know as well as I do, Cynthia Trewin, that it does not work, there is no God waiting to perform miracles when all is lost.*

'Did you get any professional help at all?' Krystina asked.

'My doctor used to call at the house every so often for the first few months. Of course, Tressa was born three months after, a month premature ... '

'You had another daughter, then?' I said and added, "That must have been some consolation.'

Krystina looked up sharply, surprised; but Cynthia Trewin seemed unperturbed. If her next few words were a rebuke, it was gently done.

'Well, one child can't replace another,' she said, 'but a new baby keeps you busy. It's work and work keeps you going. Tressa was an easy child – she always has been. She knew nothing of what had happened until she was much older, but not being around at the time, you can't expect her to feel the same way about Merryn.'

Krystina was totally absorbed in all that Cynthia Trewin was saying. After a short silence, she said, 'And your son …?'

'Oh, Jago, was a different matter. He was never quite the same after Merryn disappeared. They were very close. He had just turned six, a little over three years between them. She would follow him around at home, talking non-stop, she was a right little chatterbox. If she woke up in the night, she would go to his room, not ours, and we would find them fast asleep together next morning. He never minded, he always liked to think he was looking after her; he had a very caring nature. When she disappeared he was inconsolable and for a long time thought he was to blame. We explained to him, time and time again, that it was not his fault, but I'm not sure that he accepts that even now.'

I felt I had to make an effort to participate in this conversation, to appear natural, interested, 'I blamed myself when my father died and, of course, I had nothing to do with it.' I paused, took a breath, and struggled to say the words, 'Sometimes these things just happen. No one is really to blame.'

'Oh, but I am to blame, Mrs. Bentley, I am! You see, I left them on the beach. She was building a sandcastle – a sandhouse, she called it, – and wanted to put flowers in front of it, she had quite fixed ideas about the flowers, you know how they can be at that age, once they get an idea into their head. She was kneeling in front of it patting the area smooth, it was meant to be the garden. She was so absorbed in it I don't think she even noticed when I went away.'

She paused for a moment and in that short silence, which held years of memories, I knew the three of us were picturing the scene. I felt a sudden anguished pain for this woman and at that moment my eyes filled involuntarily with tears.

'And that's the last time I saw her … I should have thought. … I told Jago to keep an eye on her, make sure she didn't go in the water … ' She paused again. 'He was six, standing at the water's edge, I can see him now in his blue shorts, bucket in one hand, spade in the other. He would have noticed if she had gone into the sea. I think she wandered off, looking for flowers. I should have known better, it was my responsibility to look after them.'

'It's an easy mistake to make, many parents have done much worse.'

'Oh, I know, Krystina, but it was thoughtless. I should not have left them. And what for? Just to get some chips! Bill was away, driving a coachload up to London. They'd had a good lunch before we went to the beach and it was so hot that day! I felt heavy and tired, I couldn't face preparing more food. I thought they could have some chips on the beach, then all I had to do when we got back was to give them a drink, a quick bath, and put them to bed. Not much of an excuse is it?'

Neither Krystina nor I spoke.

Cynthia Trewin continued, speaking quietly. Krystina listened intently. I caught only snippets, something about waiting and time, then grief, grief and guilt, and the rest was lost. It seemed that the conversation was between the two of them, I just happened to be there, forced to watch, to listen, to bear witness.

'In the end, you learn to survive. I had to pull myself

together for Jago and the new baby and that prevented me from completely going under. Bill was in as bad a state as I was, of course, but somehow we just went on because there is nothing more you can do and in time you learn to live with it.

You never forget, of course. It's at Christmas, birthdays and other family gatherings, though nobody mentions it at the time, that we are all conscious of the fact that we are not quite complete. At such times, we are acutely aware of all that she has missed, the life she should have had, the life that was hers by right.

I always buy flowers for her birthday – Merryn loved flowers – and each year I press one of them in a book. I have thirty of them now – thirty for thirty Septembers. I miss her, but we are missing a child almost three years old, not a grown up woman. Although I always imagine otherwise, in reality, we probably wouldn't know her if we met her.'

'It must be very hard,' Krystina remarked.

Cynthia Trewin had been leaning forward, now she seemed to breathe deeply as she sat upright. 'Oh dear, I've been talking too much. I don't usually talk like this to strangers ...' She looked momentarily confused, 'Oh, I didn't mean that, not you, you don't seem like a stranger. Well, you're not – we met nearly two hours ago.'

She gave a little laugh and Krystina smiled.

'Sometimes, I have tried to imagine that Merryn is alive and well, that she remembers nothing of that time, that she is happy somewhere and living a normal life ...' She paused for a few moments, 'but too often, other thoughts come into mind.' She looked up and said, more strongly, forcefully, 'It's not knowing, not knowing what happened, that's the worst part.' It was the only time Cynthia Trewin had sounded emotional.

I waited for Krystina to say something, to change the conversation but she said nothing. I made an effort to speak. 'What does your son do now?'

'Jago is a potter, Mum,' Krystina said.

'Jago always had a bit of an artistic streak and that's what he wanted to do. He studied fine art and pottery at college, then he worked with one of the St.Ives potters for four years before setting up on his own in Newlyn. He lives there, in two rooms above his workshop.'

'He sounds interesting,' said Krystina.

'He was a very lively little boy, always asking questions, he had a restless sort of energy about him, but after Merryn went he became very quiet. He seemed to withdraw into himself, spent his time reading and drawing – pages and pages of drawings, thick black lines of graphite almost scarring the white drawing paper and nearly all to do with disasters – storms, shipwrecks, car crashes, that sort of thing. It was very worrying. His teacher at school encouraged him, and it clearly helped with the anger and frustration he was feeling. By the time he was in his teens he had turned that destructive energy into something positive and that's when he decided that he wanted to join the crew on the lifeboat.'

'How old is he now?' asked Krystina.

'He's thirty six. Merryn, of course, would be thirty two now. About the same age as you.' She looked at Krystina and then smiled at me. 'You see, there are still times when I notice. It's the first thing I thought when Krystina spoke to me in the

Cornishman office. It's easy to imagine a resemblance. The mind plays tricks, suddenly, when you least expect it.'

'And you're right. I was thirty two in May.'

'Merryn was born in October. Thirty three next month.'

For a moment she seemed lost in thought; thinking perhaps of that day nearly thirty three years ago and of what might have been.

'When will you know the results of the DNA tests?' Krystina asked.

'Well, the police want them as soon as possible, of course, but they have to do mitochondrial DNA testing because of the age of the remains and that can take quite a long time.'

By then we will be home, far away, I thought.

'Does your daughter live with you?' I asked.

'Tressa is married now and lives in Truro.'

'She has an unusual name.'

'It's Cornish. I gave them all Cornish names.'

'What does she do?'

'Hospital receptionist. I usually see her once a week.'

Cynthia Trewin opened her handbag and took out three or four photographs. She looked at them and then passed two to me. 'I had these left over from the newspaper office. They were taken last Christmas. This is the four of us and this one is a close up of Tressa and Jago.'

I had no choice but to look at photographs of this woman's children. I placed them on my lap as my hand trembled so much and I noted the slim bodies, the height, a little above average, the dark hair, the smile, definitely the smile, and I wondered if others would make similar comparisons.

'Do they mostly resemble you or your husband, Mrs. Trewin?' I asked as I handed them back to her.

'Oh. I'm not sure. A mixture of both of us, probably, it's hard to tell. I think Tressa looks more like her father. She's like him in many ways – sensible, reliable, she has a lot of friends. Jago and Merryn were similar, very lively, always laughing, both of them. They looked alike as well, you could tell they were brother and sister. Everybody said so.'

'Krystina takes after her father, at least in looks; she's more like me in temperament,' I said, and Krystina looked at me in surprise with a somewhat bemused expression.

'I'd really like to see some of Jago's work,' she said.

'Well, he does do some individual pieces but they are expensive and the market is limited. He mostly makes functional pots – mugs, cups, plates, pitchers, he can make a hundred or more in a day, and it's these repeat thrower items that sell. They are very attractive – he says he aims for beauty with function at affordable prices. You may find something in one or two shops here, or you could always go to his workshop. I'm sure he wouldn't mind, he's sociable enough when he meets people. In fact, I think you'd get on with him very well.' She turned to me, 'You have two children, Mrs. Bentley?'

It was not so much a question as she already knew the answer, more of an invitation to include me in the conversation. Feeling on safer ground, I answered too eagerly, too rapidly, 'Yes, I have a married son, seven years younger than Krystina. He's running the family wine business with me and lives part of the year here and part in France. Krystina also helps with the business at times, but her job at the university is very demanding. In fact, this is very much a working holiday for her, she's been writing an article on social policy and ethics and …'

'Yes, all right, Mum,' Krystina interrupted, looking uncomfortable.

'No, I understand. You must be very proud of her, Mrs. Bentley, I know I would be.' She stood up and came over to me, 'Now I really must get going. No, no, don't get up. You are not well, you're still trembling a little. I hope you feel better after a good night's rest.'

While she was speaking, she held out her hand which I had to shake. Then, as she approached the door, Cynthia Trewin noticed Krystina's painting on the cupboard. She stopped to look at it.

'This is very good. Did you do it?' she asked Krystina.

'Yes, I paint occasionally, not very often these days.'

'You did it here?'

'Yes, at Porthminster, soon after I arrived. But it could be any beach, any sandy beach with a lot of children. It was such a hot day and the beach was crowded, full of young children playing.'

'It's full of vitality … the bright colours … you've captured the playfulness very well. I've seen as many children as that playing on a beach on a hot day.'

'I just wanted to capture the impression they made on me.'

'It's an interesting impression … quite powerful actually. It's the contrast between those children and the stillness of the sea and sky, all that blue and not a boat, a cloud or a bird in sight, … it draws you into the painting. In fact, I find it a little unsettling.'

'Unsettling?' I said.

'Well, we each see different things in a painting. That's what makes it so good. Artists are like the rest of us, they tend to see what they want to see. They create their own sense of reality.' She stood back from the painting, still looking at it. 'This painting intrigues me. Have you noticed, Mrs. Bentley, there isn't a single adult here, only children.'

I had to confess I had not noticed. I had not given it the same consideration as Cynthia Trewin. She turned to go, and started to walk to the door, but as she did so she glanced once more at the painting and then stood still. Something had caught her attention, and I saw the slightly surprised expression as she looked at the picture for a little longer than was comfortable. 'It's very interesting,' was all she said before leaving the room but I could tell she was still thinking about it.

I wondered what had held her attention, but, much as I wanted to, I could not look closely at that painting again, at that calm and treacherous sea, at those children playing innocently, on sand and in water. I was afraid of what I might find.

Krystina accompanied her, insisting on giving her a lift to her sister's.

'No, it's only a twenty minute walk from here. You stay and look after your mother. I think she has a temperature, so keep an eye on her. It's been lovely meeting you and thank you for the tea.'

Krystina must have walked to the road with her because she was gone for a full ten minutes.

★

This meeting had been as excruciating as torture for me and I suffered further under those ten soundless minutes, for they would not have remained silent and I had no idea of what they said to each other.

She came in smiling and slightly breathless.

'Krystina, what was that woman doing here?' I asked, my voice little more than a whisper. I felt weak, as if part of me had dissolved.

'You won't believe it! It was quite amazing, actually. I met her in the newspaper office. She's lived in Penzance for years now, they moved there when her husband got a full time job as a travel agent. He'd had close links with the agency when he was a coach driver.

Well, after I did the photocopying, I thought I'd have a look at old newspapers. I was curious about the way the case was reported thirty years ago. So I went in to the newspaper office to ask if they had past papers that I could see or find online and, just after, who should walk in but Cynthia Trewin. I recognized her immediately, of course. Apparently, the paper had rung to ask her if they could take some more photos of the family and interview them. She said she had already made a press statement and didn't want to add anything more but she would bring one or two recent photos in to the office and they could choose which they wanted. Well, as soon as I saw her I knew I just had to speak to her.'

'So, you just introduced yourself – just like that – to a complete stranger!'

'But she didn't seem like a stranger. We've seen her on television, read about her in the paper. It's different. She was very approachable.'

'You make her sound like a celebrity! What if everyone started to talk to her?'

'But they don't. Many people avoid speaking to her. It just seemed the right thing to do, for *me* to do *then* because I was there in the office, at the same time, just the two of us. It was one of those coincidences, one of those chance encounters, that you can't ignore because …'

'Coincidences happen all the time, we read too much into them.'

'It wasn't just that. It was because we had lived in that house. We had stayed there at the same time as Merryn went missing. The murderer must have had some connection with the house if he buried her there in that garden.'

'You don't know that. I still think it's more likely that she drowned.'

'Then who else would be buried in the garden?'

I had no answer for her.

'I don't know why we're arguing about it. It seemed the right thing to do under the circumstances. And she didn't mind, in fact she seemed quite pleased that I had spoken to her. I said we hadn't been here on holiday again until now.'

'Why would she want to know that?'

'Oh, she was very interested. She, too, thought it was quite a coincidence.'

'In what way can all this be so unusual?' I asked, dismissively.

'It's obvious! We were here when the child went missing, the body was buried in the garden of the house in which we stayed. Now, thirty years later, having not been near the place since, we are here again only a few miles away and the body is discovered and, just by chance, I meet Merryn's mother. It's obviously quite a coincidence.'

'Things like this happen all the time; I can't see how it can be as significant as you are trying to make it.'

'Well it may serve to jog your memory about something you've forgotten, you never know. Coincidences or chance happenings, whatever you choose to call them, are, at least interesting and may even be significant. For all we know, they may be caused by some sort of karmic energy.'

'Oh, really, Krystina!' I almost spluttered, desperately trying to change the drift of the conversation. 'I have no time for that energy stuff and I didn't know you did either. There are no such forces directing our lives!'

She smiled and I knew she was being more than a little provocative. 'What about the sub-conscious mind? People reveal all sorts of things about themselves without realizing it. That has an influence without us *consciously* knowing or directing it.'

'That's different.'

'Not really. I'm only suggesting that we are not always so in control of our lives as we think we are; certain things like coincidences can be explained in a variety of ways.'

'All talk and supposition,' I said in a tone that implied that was all to be said about the matter.

It was, of course, unfortunate timing. I knew that, and felt that I had walked right into it by agreeing to come to Cornwall when all my instincts told me not to.

When she spoke, her voice cut into my thoughts and startled me. 'The police take notice of these things you know. At the time they even consulted a medium about Merryn's disappearance.'

I leaned forward, 'And what did she say?'

'Ah, now you're interested! The medium held some of Merryn's clothes, she had to feel them for a while before she said she saw sand and water and Merryn walking away on her own. She also saw Merryn walking back into their lives.'

'Well, that wasn't much help, was it? Anyway, there was a thorough search for her at the time. If she had been anywhere she would have been found.'

'No, it wasn't much help. It was the sort of thing anyone could have said. Although, if we did remember anything more about that garden, it could be helpful. After all, I was extremely frightened so I may have been aware of something else happening, something you did not notice. I couldn't have been that frightened of you, could I? I keep thinking there must be something else, something I have forgotten.'

'You were only two! Anyway, I've told you everything I know.'

'Well, when I remembered being scared, that was a sudden memory, dragged up from my sub-conscious by the sight of that tree. You may remember something too, quite suddenly. Several people have given all sorts of information this week, there have been two reported sightings of Merryn, although how that is possible after thirty years, I don't know.'

'People imagine all sorts of things. The Trewins shouldn't take too much notice of what some people imagine.'

'Oh, she knows that well enough, she seems quite level-headed; but you never know when a memory or chance observation may lead somewhere.'

'So, how did she get to be here, in this cottage?'

'She said she was going to St. Ives to see her sister so I

offered to give her a lift. She's quite interesting to talk to so when we got here…'

I interrupted her. 'And what did you talk about while you were driving here? It must have taken a good twenty minutes.'

'Oh, she talked about the family, where they lived, this part of Cornwall. I told her about us, our work, the vineyard, that sort of thing. She was very interested and asked a lot of questions about wine. Anyway, when I got here I invited her in for a cup of tea. And just five minutes later you came in and gave us a fright.'

'Yes, I'm sorry about that. I'm not sure what came over me.'

'Cynthia thought you had a slight temperature.'

Cynthia! Cynthia!

'You seem to be on very familiar terms very suddenly and how does she know I have a temperature?'

'Just observation, I suppose. She's used to dealing with people, she's a pharmacy assistant. Perhaps you were just over-tired, but you must promise me you'll go for a check up as soon as you get home. You haven't been quite yourself for the past couple of weeks.'

To please her, I promised and she made some food and that evening we watched television. Krystina seemed happy and relaxed. Every so often she made some speculative remark about the Trewins. I said no more about them. I wanted to hear no more about them. I was anxious and could eat little. I waited until it was late enough to say I was tired and I went to bed. Soon we would be gone, far away from Cornwall and Cynthia Trewin.

I could not get her out of my mind and I took a long time to fall asleep and when I did the dream returned.

We were standing on the beach, where the sea met the rocks. He kissed me. 'I love you,' he said, 'I'll never let you go.' 'I won't let you,' I said. I watched him running away along the beach. Then he turned and shouted, 'Until tomorrow!' The sea rose to my knees, my thighs, I stood on tiptoe as Mark turned in the distance and we waved and in my dream we waved and waved and I could not stop until I felt the water up to my waist so I let myself float on my back in the water, watching him disappear from sight. Then I flipped over to swim to the cove and woke in terror.

12

Next morning Krystina brought me tea in bed. 'I think you should take it easy today; you may have been overtired yesterday. Why not get up late and stay in, I'll do the cooking, perhaps a short walk along the beach later on, we can read or watch television.'

'No. no. I'm quite well, Krystina. I'd like to go out, go away somewhere. Did you enquire about that trip to the Scilly Isles?'

'Yes, no problem, the boat leaves in the morning. I was going to ask you, but after you almost fainted I thought we ought to stay here and take it easy.'

'Nonsense! I'm quite well! And to tell you the truth, I was looking forward to going over to the islands. I've never been there before; it will be a new experience.'

It would be a distraction, because that is what I wanted. To be away from here, far from the television, Cynthia Trewin and Krystina's comments about the family.

'Well, if you're really sure, if it wouldn't be too much for you …'

'No, no, it won't be too much. I doubt if we'll find a hotel at such short notice but a B and B for a couple of nights may be a possibility, you never know. It would be nice to visit some of the islands.'

Krystina left me with my morning tea and spent the next half hour on the phone before announcing, 'We sail tomorrow morning and I've managed to get a hotel on St. Mary's for three nights.'

'Oh, that's wonderful, darling. It gives us time to get ready. I'm really looking forward to it.' I almost bounced out of bed to show her how well I was and headed for the shower.

I was relieved. Three days on St. Mary's, then three more days here and it would be time to go home and leave Cornwall, for me forever; for Krystina, at least a year, and by then she may have formed an attachment to some other place, either here or abroad. I would do my best to expedite it. My mind was busy making plans about where to go, faraway places I could entice her to as I had done before.

We sailed on a mild sea with fair weather and our hotel met all expectations.

Though I prefer hills and moors and long country walks, Krystina loved the islands and because she was happy and absorbed in our activities I was content. She mentioned the Trewins only once.

'I wonder how they are?' she mused on the second day as we were walking on Tresco. 'How long do you think the DNA tests will take?'

'I really have no idea. These things take time. And we have to think of having lunch sometime soon. It's gone one o'clock.'

'Yes, we'll eat soon. Their son sounds interesting, he seems to be a bit of a recluse, doesn't he?'

143

'He probably prefers his own company, a lot of people do. It's not so unusual. Now, I really do think we should walk a little faster. I'm getting quite hungry.'

She said no more about them and we ate our meal in peace before visiting the Abbey Gardens and Cromwell's Castle. I began to enjoy our time there: the circular boat trips to the islands, the Bishop Rock Lighthouse, the seals and puffins and our walk at low tide, across the sandbar, from one island to another; the leisurely walk along the coastal path on St. Mary's, where salty sea spray and the scent of hedgerow flowers seemed to cleanse and soothe.

The events over the past week had left me anxious and tired, but the warm breezes which blew across the sea seemed to blow away my worries and I fell under the illusion that we were far away from the Trewins, instead of being only thirty miles from the mainland.

We arrived back in the late afternoon, and soon after we were back in the cottage, I showed Krystina every photograph I had taken on my camera and talked incessantly about the trip.

'You really liked the islands, didn't you?' she said.

'Oh, I loved it there – quiet, peaceful, far from the madding crowd and all that.'

She laughed. 'Next year, we'll stay longer, maybe for a week, perhaps two weeks. We could book ahead now. What do you think?'

'Oh, I don't know. We don't know where we'll be this time next year. There may be other places, other islands we could visit. I hear the Hebrides are quite interesting and everyone says the Isle of Skye is beautiful.'

'Well, maybe, it's a possibility,' she said slowly, 'although,

I am serious about coming back here, a small flat would do, just for an occasional break, long weekends, that sort of thing, not necessarily next year, but perhaps sometime in the next couple of years.'

We went to bed soon after and got up late the next morning. Only two more nights, forty eight hours to go and we would be going home. I suggested that we make the most of the time left and visit certain places.

'Tintagel is worth visiting and we could stop at Padstow for lunch,' I said. 'How about Port Isaac?'

'You're very keen to see more of Cornwall. You've always thought it over rated.'

'Well, now we're here, we should make the most of it,' I replied brightly.

'I agree! And we shall. We could go across the moors at Bodmin today and to Tintagel tomorrow. But first, I'll go and get some milk and eggs and perhaps some salad stuff for tonight. We can eat out for lunch.'

So she left for the shop and I gathered up the breakfast dishes and began to get ready to go out.

It was then that the telephone rang.

'Oh, hello, Mrs. Bentley. It's Cynthia Trewin here. Are you feeling better?'

I said I was much better, thank you.

'And did you enjoy your trip to the Scilly Isles?'

It annoyed me that she seemed to know everything about where we were and what we were doing; but I answered calmly and made a few pleasantries about our trip.

'Actually, I phoned to speak to Krystina, I said I would let her know if I had any news.'

'Oh, I'm afraid Krystina isn't here,' I said. 'She has already left and I'm just clearing things up before leaving later.'

'Oh, I thought she was leaving on Saturday. I was hoping that she'd have time to meet the family before leaving.' I could hear the disappointment in her voice.

'Well, I shall leave on Saturday, that is when we vacate the cottage, but Krystina had to leave early. The university phoned yesterday about an important meeting – it's been brought forward – something to do with student applications.'

'Oh, I'm so sorry I missed her. Well, some things can't be helped, can they? I do hope we'll see her another time, she said she'll be coming back again. Perhaps, Mrs. Bentley, you could give her a message for me.'

'Yes, of course, Mrs. Trewin,'

'Tell her we've had some news about the tests.'

My heart started to thud loudly in my chest. 'Yes, I'll tell her …. and …. and … ' I could not bring myself to say more.

'The body buried in the garden is not Merryn's.'

'Oh, I see.' I struggled, searching for words.

'I still have Merryn's clothes and shoes here, in a suitcase. Her shoes would be too big for the feet of the child, almost by two sizes. Then there's something that doesn't quite fit about the teeth. One of Merryn's milk teeth, near the back, on the bottom row, wasn't straight; it was causing problems, so the dentist decided to take it out. '

I was quite unable to speak.

'The police are convinced that the DNA results will confirm that the body buried in the garden is not Merryn's and they are extending their investigation to find the identity of the child buried there. They haven't ruled out the possibility of finding another body or even more than one. It's very worrying.'

I heard the note of worry in her voice and a few seconds passed before I managed to say, 'I will tell Krystina as soon as I get home and see her.'

'Thank you, Mrs. Bentley, and tell her that they are still questioning Mr. Evans, the owner of the house which you stayed in. He's in an old people's home but his mind is quite sharp and he remembers the events of that week and the houses he searched. Anyway, I won't keep you any longer. Tell Krystina I'm sorry I didn't manage to see her before she left.'

'Yes, I will, Mrs Trewin, and she will be sorry to have missed your call. She had to leave in a hurry; it was quite unexpected, you know how these things are.'

'Oh, I know, her work is very important. She is such a lovely young woman, your daughter, I'm so pleased to have met her. Perhaps I'll see her again if she comes back next year. I hope you have a good journey back, Mrs. Bentley.'

'Thank you and I will tell Krystina you called. Goodbye.'

'Goodbye.'

That ended our conversation and I put the phone down. There was no need to speak to her again, not ever. Cynthia Trewin was out of our lives. I sat down and breathed slowly and deeply. It was a warm day but I felt cold and it was a while before I stopped shivering.

Krystina came in some twenty minutes later and put the shopping in the fridge.

'Right! Are we ready to go?'

I was ready and couldn't leave quickly enough and we set off for Bodmin and the moors.

It was a pleasant enough day although my mind was far from the sights I was supposed to be admiring. I chatted away, at times, incessantly; at other times finding it impossible to say more than a one syllable word.

'Do you really like the place?' Krystina asked at one point, 'or are you just trying to please me?'

'Oh, I do like it, it's very interesting, it's of another age, wild and timeless and the air, the air is so … so … fresh…'

Krystina looked at me and smiled. 'You're also quite tired. Let's go and have some tea.'

We returned quite late and I said I would go straight to bed. I hoped Krystina would as well, but she said she would stay up a little longer to go through some papers. About an hour later I heard the sound of the television.

Soon after she came into my room. 'Mum? Mum, are you still awake? The police are looking for another missing child! It's all over the news. They don't think it's Merryn Trewin who's buried there.'

I did not sleep at all that night and rose early in the morning. One day more, then we could go, The ordeal was coming to an end. Krystina had gone to bed late the previous evening. She had talked about this recent news, the extent of the police search for witnesses, wondering how the Trewins were feeling, wondering what would happen next. In the end, I had said that I needed some rest; things like this happen, we must be grateful that they don't happen to us.

I had had enough. She had no idea how tight my nerves were strained. If she thought me unfeeling for the Trewins, unconcerned about her own interest in the case, I could do nothing about it. I only wanted to get us both as far away from here as possible.

Next morning she came into the kitchen as I was laying the table for breakfast.

'I'm really looking forward to visiting Tintagel. King Arthur, Round Table, Knights in shining armour, and all that. How many grains of truth are in it, do you think?' I said quite cheerily.

'All myth and legend; but it will be atmospheric and impressive; all of which is good for the imagination and the tourist industry.'

I laughed. 'Muesli? Yoghurt? Tea?'

'Oh, muesli and some tea, thanks.' She sat down at the table and watched as I poured the tea. 'I wonder how the Trewins feel now that they know the results?'

I was exasperated. 'Krystina, we are going out for our last day trip. There is nothing at all we can do to help the Trewins. Let's just concentrate on the last day of our holiday.'

She looked at me closely, slightly puzzled, but when she spoke her voice was even. 'You're right and we'll go soon.'

After we had finished breakfast, we went to our bedrooms to get ready and when I returned, ready to go, I saw her in the garden on her mobile phone. She must have been speaking for several minutes and when she had finished the conversation, she stood staring at the ground for several seconds before walking straight for the back door.

'Right! Are we ready to go?' I said, picking up my coat.

'No, we are not!' She stood there, angry and incredulous. 'I have just phoned Cynthia to say I had heard the news on television last night and she said she phoned to let me know yesterday. Why didn't you tell me she had phoned?'

'What? Cynthia Trewin? Oh, yes, so she did. I must have forgotten to tell you.'

'How could you forget when I told you the news last night? Why didn't you say, 'Yes, I know, she phoned, I forgot to tell you'? Why didn't you?'

'Well, there wasn't much point then, was it? You already knew.'

'That is quite beyond the point! She phoned! She left a message! You deliberately withheld that from me. And you told her I wasn't here, that I had already left.' She spoke quietly and precisely as if she were giving some important evidence which could not be misconstrued.

I could not think of anything remotely plausible to say. She was pale and tense, yet there was as much puzzlement as anger in her voice as she asked, with mounting desperation, 'Why? Why? Why?'

'Krystina, you are getting worked up over nothing.' I spoke slowly, trying to keep my voice calm.

Her voice rose, 'I am worked up! And it's not over nothing! You concoct some story that I have suddenly left Cornwall, leaving you here all on your own to clear up! Lies! Why? I don't understand!'

I sat down, shaken, aware that my hands were trembling. I did not know what to say.

'You're hiding something from me, aren't you? Something you won't tell me. I know you are!' She paused for several seconds, seconds which seemed like minutes, before continuing. 'You haven't shown any interest, not one ounce of understanding for the Trewins. You can't bear me mentioning Cynthia's name.' There was another pause.

'You're not usually like this, so ... so ... *un*empathetic about people, so, so, *indifferent*, no, not even that, *hostile,* actually *hostile* about a mother who's lost a child and another child who was buried in a garden, where we stayed. It's not an Agatha Christie story, it's *real* and it's horrible. And you are being very devious about it, not passing on messages, telling outright lies ...'

'It was too upsetting!' I blurted out, 'I didn't want you involved.'

'Involved in what, for God's sake?'

'Krystina, do calm down! Being interested in people who are in the news is quite understandable, but you were developing a morbid interest in the case, you seem to have been preoccupied with it.'

'That is absolute rubbish! You know it is! I met Cynthia Trewin, she's not a complete stranger. We had lived in the house during the time her daughter went missing. A body was found buried there ....'

'Enough! Enough! I can't stand it any more! It's making me ill!' I shouted, unable to stop myself.

Krystina looked shocked and said nothing. There was an uncomfortable silence as I breathed deeply, trying to compose myself.

My voice, when I spoke, was unsteady. 'Merryn Trewin drowned in the sea, her body was never found. You need to understand that. It's very sad, of course, but it's not such an unusual occurrence, the sea claims lives every year here. It's only natural for the Trewins to hope she is still alive although in my opinion that is nothing more than wishful thinking.'

'So you keep saying. There's no evidence that she went into the sea. The Trewins are not alone in thinking that

Merryn may have been abducted, the police think so too. In which case, she could still be alive somewhere.'

'Merryn Trewin is dead,' I said flatly.

'You almost want her to be! You are being perverse! We don't *know* if she's dead. She *could* be alive, it's possible. *Her* body has not been found, but another one has, in that garden, near that tree …..'

'That has nothing to do with it! It was buried in the garden either long before she was drowned or long after. The two events are not related.'

'The police seem to think they are, it's too much of a coincidence.' She looked at me, waiting, before saying somewhat dismissively, 'Oh, but I forgot! You don't believe in coincidences, do you? Maybe you should tell them, you seem to know more about it.'

I ignored the sarcasm. 'Everyone is jumping to conclusions. It's a simplistic way of thinking. Anyway, whether they are connected or not, it has absolutely nothing to do with us.'

Krystina was thoughtful for a few moments. When she spoke, her voice was calm.

'So, if this has nothing at all to do with us, why didn't you pass on the message? Why did you say I had gone away?'

'I wanted to protect you.'

'That's ridiculous! What do you think you're protecting me from?'

'From yourself! Your interest is unwholesome and it's spoiling your holiday. It is not good for you, Krystina. As for myself, the story has stirred old memories. I hated it here, couldn't wait to get away.'

She sat thinking for a while, clearly puzzled.

'I don't understand you, I really don't. Your reaction is irrational. Something isn't right.'

I could hear the clock ticking in the silence which followed, a silence which felt like an accusation and I was too afraid to break it; I had said too much already. Soon, she would speak again, there would be another observation, another question and I was afraid of what she might say. I stood up abruptly, walked out of the room and into the bedroom. I was trapped, like a defenceless animal, in a snare of my own making, and I could do nothing.

Twenty minutes must have passed before Krystina came into the bedroom. She sat down beside me on the bed and spoke gently. 'There's something you're not telling me. I can tell. You're not yourself. Wouldn't it help if you told me?'

'I've told you all I know. What more can I say?'

'Perhaps you saw something …. suspected something … didn't report it ….'

'What do you mean? I saw something! What was there to report? What are you suggesting?' I spoke quickly, agitated.

'I'm not suggesting anything. You know very well I'm not saying you had anything to do with it. You *know* I'm not saying that. I'm only saying there's something you're not telling me and I have no idea why not.'

'There's no more to tell,' I sad flatly.

'But it is to do with the Trewins, isn't it?'

'No. It's your obsession with them.'

'I'm not obsessed with them,' she said calmly and paused for a few seconds before continuing, 'I am interested, perhaps *intrigued* is a better word. And I am curious about your reaction to them.'

I was silent.

'I know you haven't been quite yourself while you've been here. You were not well when Cynthia was here. You had quite a turn when you got back from your walk. It seemed like a shock. Of course, a hot day, a ten mile walk … I don't know how you had time to walk so far, you must have walked like a galloping horse.'

Her tone was light but the irony was intended and invited a response. I did not reply.

'Tell me what is wrong, Mum. I know there's something, something you don't want me to know.' She put her arm around my shoulder. 'Just tell me.'

And this was the moment, the invitation for revelation, the moment in time which would change everything.

'Nothing. There's nothing to tell.'

She smiled, not unsympathetically, and waited, still hoping I would say something. Then, with a sigh, she stood up, moved towards the door. 'I think I'll go into Penzance to see Cynthia. At the moment I'm likely to get more response from her than I am from you. Anyway, I said I would try to see her again before I left. I feel I ought to go.'

'But, what about Tintagel? We're ready to go.'

'I don't feel like going now. Would you mind going without me?' It was more of a statement than a question. 'Cynthia said she'd like me to meet the rest of her family and I'd really like to meet them. There are questions … '

'But this is absurd! You hardly know the woman! This …' I searched for words, clutching at straws, almost frantic in my attempt to stop her from going, '… this shop assistant pharmacist, you don't even know her family! What, the coach driver husband, the receptionist, the boy who's a potter, a semi recluse? What on earth have you got in common with these people?'

She looked at me, shocked and speechless; but when, after several seconds, she did speak, her voice was low. 'Can you hear yourself? I can't believe what you just said. You sound like a stranger. What's got into you?'

'Nothing's got into me other than your morbid fascination which I can't understand. It's excessive.'

'It's not excessive. It's only natural to feel some interest, a measure of sympathy with the family. If it had happened to you…'

'I hope I would have accepted that it was an accident, grieved properly, and moved on.' My words, cold and heartless, hid quite different feelings that were coursing through me. Inwardly, I was crumbling, collapsing.

'But they don't know what happened and they are not responsible for it hitting the headlines again this year. Actually, Cynthia is taking this quite calmly and sensibly. You are the one who is reacting, and reacting quite aggressively.'

'You don't know her or her family.'

'I do know her, she came here one afternoon, remember? I phoned her from the Scilly Isles and she said she hoped I'd call and meet them before I went back.'

'Why on earth would you want to? They're strangers, you have nothing to do with them, nothing at all.'

'There you go again! You are just too concerned about having anything to do with them. You actually *resent* the fact that I met her, invited her here. Actually, if you want to know, at first, I was just being polite and then she seemed pleased that I had spoken to her. Sometimes you just meet someone and find they're easy to get on with. It's called human interaction and that's what we have in common, we are both human beings. Does that answer your question?'

'There's no need to be supercilious.'

She went to the window and stood there looking out for a while. 'Anyway, I like her, she's been very pleasant and friendly. There's only today or tomorrow morning and we won't have time then. So I think I'll go now.'

'Now? Today? You're going to leave me on my own, the last day of the holiday?'

'Yes. I told her I would drive over this morning. It's the right thing to do, especially after you told her I had already left. You see, I don't really mind mixing with coach drivers, receptionists, boy potters.'

She must have instantly regretted the sarcasm for she continued in a softer tone, 'Would you like to come with me?'

'Of course not! You know very well I can't!' I snapped. 'And you shouldn't go either. It's ... it's not appropriate ... no good will come of it.' I stopped as I saw the look of incomprehension cross her face and the hollow feeling in my stomach intensified as I thought of the day ahead and I could not fail to hear the note of pleading which crept into my voice as I said, 'You shouldn't go now either, it won't make any difference to them, it won't do any good. Stay with me, we'll have a nice day out, the last day, just the two of us ...'

'Now you're being pathetic,' she said matter of factly. 'I have to see them today, it's the right thing to do after you ...' She did not continue for a moment and I hoped she was about to change her mind but she said, 'I feel I owe it to them ... anyway, I *want* to.'

'Then I'll stay here on my own if you insist on going there.'

She took her painting off the cupboard and reached for her bag.

'What are you doing with that?'

'Cynthia said she'd like to see it again. When I said I'd see her later this morning, she asked if I could bring it with me, if it wasn't too much trouble.'

'She saw it here. Why would she want to see it again?'

'She said she wanted Jago to see it.'

'Why?'

'I really don't know.' She spoke wearily, tired of questions. 'Perhaps she thinks he'd be interested. Perhaps she just likes it, that's all, and if she likes it that much, I'll give it to her. Now I really must go. I'll see you later.'

She said no more, placed the painting under one arm, picked up her bag and her car keys and left. From the window I watched her drive away, until the car was out of sight.

I stood there for several minutes, completely alone. I shivered, cold with fear, as another wave of foreboding rippled through me.

I was losing her, losing her to Cynthia Trewin.

13

I had made a mistake with the phone call, a foolish impulsive mistake. I should have known better. There was nothing now I could do, but wait. Perhaps she would return soon. How long did she need to say goodbye to the Trewins? Some words, expressions of concern, polite interest, a cup of tea, what, half an hour? An hour? More? Not much more, surely. She could be home by eleven, midday, at the latest, and all may yet be well, I told myself.

She phoned soon after ten that morning and I rose from the chair, the first time since she left, to answer it.

'Oh, you haven't left yet? I just wanted to let you know I'm staying at the Trewins for the day. Cynthia wants me to meet the family and Jago is coming round later and they've asked me to stay for the evening meal.'

I felt sick. 'I'll drive up to Tintagel, as we planned, and when I get back, I'll get things ready for tomorrow and have an early night.'

'O.K. if that's what you'd like to do, perhaps it's for the best. I'll probably be back quite late tonight.'

There was nothing much I could say to this and I only suggested that she didn't stay too late as we had a long drive the following day.

'There's another reason I phoned. The police have appealed for witnesses, and they're trying to trace everyone who was known to have stayed in Pensquidden Terrace between twenty eight and thirty two years ago. Their investigation is well underway, they have several statements already.'

'How do you know all this?'

'Cynthia told me. They reckon it will involve well over a hundred people and I imagine they'll be questioning some of them again, when they've got the DNA results from the skeleton.'

'What, will they want everyone's DNA?"

'Well, not everyone's. I suppose it depends on who was there and when and what they find. It will help them to eliminate people from their investigations. At the moment, the bag the body was wrapped in may be significant because it wasn't made in this country, so perhaps they're thinking it belonged to a foreigner or a traveller. That Mr. Evans you mentioned remembers searching the houses at the time, and he remembers two men sharing one house and a woman and young child another, and that must be us, just like you said. I thought we could see the police tomorrow just before going home.'

'But I can't tell them anything. I didn't notice anything. Have you spoken to the police? Have you told them we were there?'

'No, I haven't seen them. Of course, I haven't. They wouldn't be interested in me, I was only a child. But you will have to see them, just for the record. It's nothing to worry about. It's just personal details, your name, address, dates we were at Pensquidden Terrace, residence before and after, and then anything at all you remember, anyone calling at the house, anything unusual. It's just basic, routine stuff. It will only take a few minutes and tomorrow morning is the only time we have left.'

My throat felt dry and when my lips moved no sound came out. Everything was unravelling. I was stunned and more frightened than I had been for thirty years.

'Mum, are you still there? ... Mum? Can you hear me?'

'Yes, of course. I said that's a good idea.'

'Oh, I didn't hear you. Are you all right?'

'Yes, I'm fine. I'm about to leave for Tintagel. I'll probably be in bed by the time you get back.'

'Well, make the most of today. See you tonight.'

I put the phone down and stared out of the window. Tension held my body rigid; I was stone cold, as frozen as a statue. Time was catching up on me and I knew I was on the brink of an abyss which opened like the jaws of hell before me. I needed to get far away from here. I had to think, to plan, and to make contingency arrangements.

This realization brought me suddenly to life. Hastily, I packed all my clothes in a suitcase, and wrote a note for Krystina.

I am going home today. It's for the best.

She would find it late that evening. By that time I would be three hundred miles away. In the morning she would have to pack, see the landlord and return the keys of the property before she could leave. At that point she would phone me to let me know what time she would be back. She always did, it was a habit established in her teenage years. I had more than 24 hours ahead of me. It would give me time.

I left for the long drive home, stopping only once in Dorset at a service station for petrol. I bought a paper and read it while I drank a coffee. Half way down the third page I read:

CORNISH MYSTERY INTENSIFIES.
The remains of a young child found in a shallow grave in the garden of a holiday cottage have not yet been identified. Police are questioning…

I read no further. It had reached the national press. Until now, few people outside of Cornwall had ever heard of Merryn Trewin. Her disappearance had never reached the national press, to some it had been just another drowning, another body lost at sea. Now, with the discovery of a child's body in a secret grave, the hunt will be on for another missing child and wild theories about what may have happened to both will be imagined and there will be some who will speculate, with macabre relish, that there may be more bodies waiting to be found.

Some stories remain local. Unimaginable horrors are with us all the time, in towns and cities, little villages, seaside places, the hills and valleys of our green and pleasant land, and only a few, a very few, get into the daily papers and capture the popular imagination. Now, on page three of a national newspaper, the story would be followed up. Soon, other papers would follow, journalists sensed a good drama and the ingredients were there – a dead child, perhaps two, maybe

161

more, grieving parents, crime, mystery. The police would make statements, people would be interviewed, the Trewins would be there, this time on a bigger stage, no doubt thinking that yet more publicity would somehow help them to retrieve what was lost or, in the modern parlance of the word, bring some sort of closure.

I had to decide what to do. There were few options open to me. There would be the police interview, a mere formality, seemingly innocuous and, much later, perhaps the possibility of a DNA test. Then there was Krystina, returning within hours from a day spent with the Trewins and what news, what revelations would she bring with her?

I thought of these things all the way home, every minute of nearly seven hours of driving. The roads were congested with traffic and roadworks, and it was nearly six when I arrived home, tense and exhausted, anxiety twisting like a corkscrew in my mind.

I poured a large whisky, and sat for a long time thinking. I had mismanaged everything. Why had I been so vague and evasive? When asked where we had stayed thirty years ago, I should have named a place, a place far from Pensquidden Terrace. Newquay would have been suitable. We could have gone there, I could have found a road near the sea and said, "One of these houses; the one in the middle"; and "No, we didn't travel around, we stayed there all the time." I could have said the tree was similar to one in Australia where she had been frightened once by a stray dog, she would have believed it. I could have shown a reasonable interest in the Trewins, behaved like a normal, rational human being and not incited her frustration, anger and suspicion.

Had I never gone to Cornwall, none of this would have happened. I was never at ease there. Even if she had phoned me at home to ask questions, I would have had time to think. Above all, she wouldn't have been there to see me, watch my reactions, argue with me. It was being in Cornwall with her that trapped me in a snare of my own making.

Now, I had to plan for tomorrow. I could do nothing because I could not tell what was happening in Cornwall. I sat for an hour, finished the whisky and went straight to my bedroom, took off my shoes, and, as I was, got into bed, pulled the bed clothes up close around me and fell asleep.

PART THREE

14

I lean back and float, gazing into the distance where Mark waves for the last time and disappears. I feel the clear sea water around me, soft and cool on my skin, my legs and arms keep me gently and effortlessly afloat. I am safe, invulnerable, alive in a way that I have not been before and it is love that has flooded my being as surely as the blood flows easily in my veins. I have everything anyone could ever want and the expectation of happiness and fulfillment which only a few ever achieve.

I swim on my back for a few slow strokes, turn over and am carried, almost effortlessly by a cool, buoyant tide, towards the shore. In less than twentyfour hours, we will be together again. We will swim, play and build sandcastles until the light fades into evening and it is time to eat together and for Krystina, tired out, to go to bed. Then the evening will slowly stretch into night for the two of us, blissfully lying in each other's arms – and at this point I notice that the little beach is deserted. The family has gone. When did they go? Why didn't I see them pass the rocks? The tide is in much further; I knew that when I walked in past the rocks. But to my left, the tide has swept into the cove, with rolling white waves far up the side of the cliff. I see the small cave where I left our clothes; they will be dry, the tide has not reached them yet. I look for Krystina but do not see her.

My arms flail the water I kick hard powerfully and water splashes around me my feet touch the sand and I rush stumbling on to the beach and I can see the top of the sandcastle but half of it is submerged under water and I run my heart beating wildly while the sand sucks my feet down and I force my legs forward forward towards the place where I have left our clothes and as I reach it I look and I call Krystina Krystina and I don't see her and I look up and down the beach and I go to the small cave a space of only a few feet and she's not there I don't know where to look I don't know what to do and I think she has left and gone to find me she has walked past the rocks and even now is on the main part of the beach where it is still safe and she is lost lost because I am not there but I can go back I can find her and then I see the top of the sandcastle again and there is a splash of yellow something floating or stuck there in the water in front of what is left of the sandcastle and I run I run and I think I hear someone screaming and I look as I run but no one is there and then I see her she is there in her yellow swimsuit face down in the water and I fall on my knees and the water is up to my thighs and I pick her up she is heavy and I scream help help help me is anyone there I need help and I listen but there is only the lap of the water and a cool wind blowing gently across the sea and I carry her up near our clothes to dry sand and I thump her back three four times and water comes out of her mouth and I speak to her say her name again and again and I put her on her back and I breathe through her mouth

168

air into her lungs and I press hard on her heart and I am counting one two three four five six seven eight nine ten eleven twelve and I breathe into her mouth again twice and I begin the heart compressions again one two three four five six seven eight nine ten eleven twelve and again and on and on again and minutes pass and I stop and put my ear to her chest but I can hear no heartbeats and she does not breathe and I speak to her Krystina wake up Krystina speak to me Krystina breathe please start breathing and then I start again again and again until I feel faint and collapse over her and I feel the sea reaching us as the tide continues its relentless course and the light has changed and I know I am too late and I look up the sky a pale grey a trail of thin white clouds passing over a pale insipid moon and all warmth has gone and I gaze into a vast emptiness and I plead with it bring her back please please please I will do anything and in this moment I believe in God because there is nothing left nothing can help us it is my only hope and I strike a bargain save her bring her back I will do anything anything anything I'll give it all away all my money everything but Krystina isn't breathing she is pale and still and cold and I offer more with every fibre of my being take me instead this is my fault not hers it's only fair just bring her back and let me die please please please do this for me for her for us.

15

I wake and am pulled abruptly into the present. It is past midnight and it is thirty years later. The dream, for the first time, has taken me past those rocks. It has taken me past them into that cove and the shock, the panic, I felt that day is with me again. I have seen my child, touched her, spoken to her. I have relived the horror. Grief and remorse consume me now as they did that day and the days and long weeks and months that followed.

She was dead. I sat beside her and cried desperate tears. I will die here too, I thought. The tide seeped up around us and I waited.

It was some time before I realized it would come no further, it had reached its course. I put on my dress over my bikini, put on my sandals and I put everything else in the beach bag. I wrapped Krystina in the large bath towel, lifted her into my arms and carried her down to the rocks which jutted into the sea at the end of the cove. Here the water was waist deep, but I managed to scramble along by the rocks, gripping them with one hand to pull us up and keep our heads out of the water as the waves dashed me against them. My arm and leg were scratched and cut, blood trickled down as I reached the beach, now deserted as families had long gone home to their teas.

I saw two boys, half way across the beach. I would ask them to help me, to call an ambulance; but as I approached they saw my wet clothes and they shouted, 'What, you got caught by the tide? Got your clothes wet, didya? We can see through your dress!' And they ran off, laughing, jeering. I walked on, all the way across the beach and then up the lane until I came to Pensquidden Terrace.

Next door, Mrs. Goodman was carrying a box to the boot of the car. Mr. Goodman had the bonnet of the car up and was checking the oil. They were getting ready to leave the next morning. I would tell them. They would know what to do.

Mrs. Goodman looked up as I approached and I saw the expression of concern that passed across her face. She came over to the fence.

'Claire! What happened? You're wet through! Oh, you're bleeding! Your arm is scratched!'

'The tide,' I said, 'we were in the cove … I didn't notice … we got cut off … Krystina was making a sandcastle … the tide came in … the rocks … '

'It's the spring tide, dear, you have to be careful at this time of month.' She gazed at me, clearly shocked by my appearance. 'Look at you, you're as white as a ghost! You're all done in.'

'Krystina …' I began, lowering my arms so that she could see her as tears overwhelmed me.

Mrs. Goodman merely glanced at Krystina, cold and still, seemingly asleep, wrapped in a beach towel, in my arms, before looking back at me, her voice soothingly comforting. 'Oh, don't you get upset, my dear. She's tired out, dear little thing, it's been a long, hot day for her and it's gone nine o'clock, way past her bedtime. She'll sleep well tonight and in the morning she'll be as right as rain. Don't you worry, children are quite tough.'

I felt her hand on my arm, a consoling gesture meant to soothe and reassure. Tears ran down my face. I could not bring myself to tell her.

'You look after yourself, now. You've had a nasty shock. Now, go in and put Krystina to bed, have a nice hot bath and a cup of tea. Cover that arm up and go to bed, get a good night's sleep. You'll feel better in the morning.'

'Yes, I will,' I heard myself say, 'I'll see you in the morning, Mrs. Goodman.'

'We're leaving early in the morning, but we'll say goodbye before we go.'

As I walked to the door I heard her say to her husband. 'She's had a fright, you can tell that. A narrow escape, if you ask me. And that little child is worn out, she looked dead to the world.'

Once in the house, I went to the bathroom where I washed the sand and the salt from her hair and her skin. I put on her clean, pink nightdress and carried her, wrapped in my arms to my bed. There I placed her, lying as she used to lie, on her side, knees raised, my little sleeping angel. I crawled in beside her, put my arms around her, drew her in close to me, as if warmth from my body would breathe new life into hers and fell into a deep and dreamless sleep.

I must have slept for more than ten hours. I woke to light

streaming through the window and to the sound of people next door, loading their car. I went to the window, thinking I would tell them now before they left. They would help me. They heard the window open and looked up.

'Oh, there you are! We were just going to knock the door to say goodbye,' Mrs. Goodman said cheerfully, looking up to the window, standing between the fence and the car. 'Did you sleep well?' She didn't wait for an answer but continued, 'And Krystina? She was tired out. Is she still sleeping?'

I looked back at the bed where the little lifeless body lay. I hesitated. It is sometimes difficult to say the right words.

'Yes, fast asleep,' I said.

'Ah, well, that will do her good. Tell her we said goodbye. Say goodbye to Mark. And you look after yourself and enjoy the rest of your holiday. It was so nice to meet you both. Perhaps we'll see you again, next year?'

'Yes, that would be nice. Have a good trip back.'

With that they got in the car, started the engine, waved to me from the window and drove away.

I went to the bathroom and showered until every trace of the beach was gone; some of the congealed blood was washed off my arm and it started bleeding again, I bandaged it roughly with strips torn from a pillowcase. Then I went down the stairs into the kitchen. There, shivering, weeping, I remained for the rest of the day.

★

We do not control our lives. We are governed by a series of events, coincidences, some auspicious, others malevolent. I went through them all that day, again and again, ticking them off in my mind, like a list. They all began with *If* as I tried to make sense of what had happened.

If the landlord of the Tregeagle hadn't needed an extra delivery from the brewery he would not have asked Mark to drive the van to collect it late that morning.

If he hadn't been given three hours off that afternoon Mark would not have arranged to borrow the van and meet us at the beach and I would not have directed him to the little cove, quieter, more secluded and cut off from the crowded main beach by huge rocks.

If Mark had turned up at two as expected I would not have swum out to the rocks every so often looking for him, wondering why he was so late.

If an articulated lorry had not crashed ten miles from the Tregeagle Inn, closing the road and causing a ten mile traffic jam, Mark would not have been three hours late.

If he had not been so anxious during those three hours and in that heightened emotional state had imagined life without us, he would not have run up waving and shouting, impulsively, 'Marry me!'

If we had not been so head over heels in love we would not have stayed there, not climbed on to the large flat rock, half hidden and sheltered from the beach, just to talk, kiss, be alone together for a minute or two, at least, initially, that was all that was intended.

If he did not have to be back at work by six, we would have gone to the cove, and not made the most of a few minutes alone on a rock.

If the family near us had not left the cove when they did, someone would have seen her stumble in the moat and would have helped her.

If the tide – a spring tide – had not surged ahead so quickly along the side of the cliff, if it had only crept into the cove in a straight line, I would have been back in time and she would not have drowned.

These were my *ifs,* the *ifs* to absolve me. Except they didn't, no matter how much I tried, because *if,* when Mark asked where Krystina was, I hadn't said she was making the sandcastle and there was a family nearby, and *if* we hadn't stayed on the white rock long enough to lose ourselves in love, *if* only I had just stayed with her the whole time, then she would still be alive. Three decisions: not inherently evil; but unthinking, careless, negligent. The consequences were monstrous and they damned me utterly.

Such were my thoughts then and in thinking them I became aware of the devastating predicament I was in. I had not reported the death. Any attempt to explain the delay would sound unconvincing. Questions would be asked. How could a child have drowned in a shallow moat of water? Where was I? When did I notice? What did I do? Why didn't I get an ambulance as soon as I could?

They would delve into my past, I saw it clearly: the breakdown, the violence towards the doctor, now upgraded to dangerous mental instability, a baby looked after mostly by her grandmother, the single parent, heir to a fortune, now too encumbered with a child, wanting freedom.

Why did I leave a two-year-old alone on a beach? Why had I left her alone for so long? The answer, if all details were ever revealed, would condemn me in everyone's eyes. I had left a child alone to meet a boyfriend and – *Child drowns while mother has sex* – I saw the headlines, lurid with accompanying details, *in public on a beach*, they would not say it was a secluded rock, almost a private place, far from public view, *with a man she had known for three weeks,* a sordid encounter, they would not call it love. Such revelations would be met with ridicule and contempt.

I had an alibi, a witness to the fact that I was not there when my child drowned. He, too, was involved in the tragedy for, without him, it would not have happened. Only Mark could have verified my account and in doing so he would be implicated, forced to give evidence, his reputation torn apart, not as much as mine, but enough, for he, too, knew that Krystina was left on the beach. He, too, was culpable.

I remembered him running across the beach less than twenty-four hours before, and I remembered the relief, the elation which lit up his face when he saw me. I remembered the surge of happiness I felt when I saw him. We both experienced something akin to a divine revelation and it was this, this awareness of our need for each other, which flung us together in mutual declarations of love. Nothing intruded on the intensity of that moment in time; the world existed only for us, for what, … half an hour, perhaps?

I could not tell him. What could I say? 'While we were together, …' The words mocked me even as I thought them. It was not possible for me to conceal what had happened, neither was it possible for me to reveal it. I loved him too deeply to expose him to the scandal that would blight both our lives. Whatever he may think about my deserting him, he must never know the reason why.

I thought, too, of my mother and the grief I was about to cause. After all she had gone through in the last six years: the death of her husband, a difficult, at times, willfully irresponsible daughter who had not lived up to expectations, and now the death of an adored grandchild whom she had cared for, uncomplaining, with tender devotion. And now, the suffering, the shame, the disgrace. I could not do it. She must never know. The guilt was mine. I would bear it alone.

I replaced the dressing on my arm. It still bled a little where the skin was torn. I hardly felt the pain. I wondered why I had struggled so hard with that little body in my arms, to get past the rocks. Why did I let that thoughtless instinct for self-survival betray me? Why didn't I let go, let the waves dash me into the rocks, let our bodies sink either peacefully or brutally into the water? I would have drowned with her, our deaths a tragic accident. It would have been far better that way.

I stayed in the kitchen all day and all night, dreading the moment when I would have to ascend the stairs and go into the bedroom. It was already late in the afternoon when, tired out from relentless tears and lack of sleep, I went to the bedroom, tearfully and tenderly wrapped her body in a white sheet and, so shrouded, put it carefully, snugly, as if she were asleep, into the large holdall and zipped it closed. I placed it in the built-in cupboard which served as a wardrobe in the bedroom.

I stayed in the house again that night. I neither ate nor washed. I drank tea and the remains of a bottle of wine. I fell asleep in the kitchen. I woke early, showered, washed my clothes and, by six in the morning, I left the house. I took the car from the garage and drove north, for miles and miles, not knowing where I was going, what I wanted to do, only wanting to get far away. I was unable to feel any emotion and this feeling of numbness mercifully remained with me as I drove up, out of Cornwall and into Devon and somewhere that night I stayed in a hotel.

★

I decided to go away, to disappear. I was not sure how I would do this. Those who disappeared were reported missing, people searched for them, enquiries were made. I knew only that to survive I had to leave and go where no one would follow. To this end, I phoned Diane at a time that I knew my mother would most likely be working in the shop.

'I need my documents, Diane, and Krystina's too,' I said, 'They are all in a folder in the bottom drawer of the dressing table. I'm going to pop over to France before coming back, just for a week or two. It's best to have everything with me, in case of emergencies and suchlike. There's no need to mention this to Mum, she'll only worry, she expected me back before I went over, but I'll be back in a month.'

'Of course,' she said, 'I'll post it off to you, first class, today. You sound a bit anxious. Are you all right?'

'Yes, I'm fine, we both are. I'm just a bit out of breath. There's no phone in the house and I ran to the phone box. Krystina can't wait to get back to the beach.'

Then I phoned The Tregeagle Inn.

The landlord answered the phone and I said, 'Dave, can you give Mark a message for me?'

'Of course. He was wondering where you were yesterday. He expected you here in the afternoon. In fact, he stayed on working, thinking you'd been delayed. Weren't you going out together later?'

'Yes, and I should have phoned yesterday, but we had to go home. It was all very sudden and unexpected. My mother was taken ill, she's in hospital.'

'Oh, dear, I am sorry. How is she?'

'Well, they're operating this afternoon. Tell Mark that I'll get in touch as soon as I know more. Tell him not to worry. If all goes well, I'll drive down next week for a day or two. We can sort things out then.'

'I'll tell him as soon as he comes in, don't worry. It must have been a shock for you, you don't sound like your normal self. You look after your mother and I hope she gets better soon.'

I spent the rest of the day some fifty miles away sitting on another beach, watching young people splashing and showing off in the water, parents handing out sandwiches and drinks, buying ice creams and children playing. Children seemed to be everywhere. Much as I resisted, I seemed to be inexorably pulled toward them. I scoured the beach, looking, always looking. I watched their movements, searched their faces for the faintest resemblance. I was looking for Krystina.

I thought of her timid attempts to walk in the sea, holding on to me for dear life.

'Feet,' she would say, 'no more!' And I was patient with her, 'Just a little bit more, I'm holding both your hands, you won't fall.' And after ten days, she would go in as far as her knees, still gripping my hands tightly. I looked at other children, just as young, paddling, building sandcastles although none as big, made with such haphazard care, as Krystina's. I ached with unbearable sadness.

179

16

I dared not stay away from Pensquidden Terrace for long. The landlord, or the new people who replaced the Goodmans could call and my absence could arouse concern. I drove back slowly, reluctantly, sometimes talking to Krystina as if she were still there. Once, stopping for petrol, I said, 'Would you like a drink, some milk, Krystina?' and I clearly heard her say, 'No milk. Juice.' At times, I thought I was going mad.

I arrived back very late, slept fitfully in the small bedroom and, next morning, my folder with passports, birth certificates, all that I needed, arrived. I did not know at that stage what I would do. In four days time I would have to vacate the house.

I sat thinking for a very long time the next day, while the minutes on the kitchen clock ticked away like a time bomb and the hours passed slowly turning into darkness and another long and sleepless night.

It was the following day in the afternoon, that I felt I could stay in the house no longer. At this hour Mark would be working at the Tregeagle Inn, some eight miles away, and he would think I was far away in Sussex; I knew there was no possibility of meeting him, but, even so, I went out wearing a long beach dress, a sunhat and dark sun glasses and I made my way cautiously down to the beach. 'Just look at the beach, face it again, relive each step you took that day,' I told myself, thinking that returning to it would somehow stop the persistent images which would suddenly erupt in frightening flashbacks in my mind.

I walked only so far. I do not know if people were sunbathing and swimming in that quiet, secluded cove. The rocks leading to it repelled me and I knew I could not pass them, could not look again on the passive yellow sand behind them. So I went back along the beach, merged into the happy mass of people playing and lying in the sun.

It was a hot day and this part of the beach was crowded. Some parents were in the sea with their children; some older children were playing with a ball which occasionally went into the sea and there would be a rush to stop it from floating out with the tide; younger children were digging in the sand, some were filling pails with water to pour into the holes.

Several times, seeing a young child thus occupied, I would move close, momentarily believing beyond all reason that it may be her, that I had woken from a dream, that a miracle may yet happen. I looked for Krystina in every child I saw, knowing that I would never find her. Distraught and despairing, I sat down on the sand and watched.

★

I was tired from lack of sleep and the heat of the afternoon sun, so I may have dozed off for an hour or so. When I next opened my eyes I noticed a boy, about five or six years old, carrying a bucket, standing where the waves rippled across the sand. As they retreated he bent down, scooped something up and put it in the bucket. Then he walked towards a child who appeared to be building a strangely shaped sandcastle. He stood over her, talking. She looked up at him briefly, said something, then returned with absorbed attention to her work. And in that moment, she could have been Krystina. She reminded me so much of her, the same engrossed concentration, the same age, the same dark brown hair … I almost leapt up and rushed to her. I wished … I wished so much …. if only … I eased myself forward so I could hear them.

'You can decorate it with these. I can get some more.'

'I don't want shells,' she said, patting the sides of an almost square block of sand she had made.

 I was captivated as I watched them both; the boy just standing there, the girl smoothing the sand in front of the construction she was building. Soon, a woman approached and started talking to them. She wore knee length beach shorts and a baggy top, a little overweight I thought. Her back was towards me, it was hard to hear her. I moved forward a few inches. She seemed to be remonstrating with the girl.

'You'll have to make do with the shells. Sandcastles don't have flowers.'

'It's not a sandcastle! It's a house!' the child declared. 'Houses have flowers!'

'Well, flowers don't grow on sand. They grow in gardens.'

'You can get some dandelions back on the path, there's some grass there,' said the boy.

'The shells will look very nice on the house, you don't

need flowers,' said the woman. She turned to the boy. 'Now don't let her go in the water, Jago, not until I get back. The fish and chip shop is open now, you can have some chips on the beach. I'll only be ten minutes. You can paddle, but no deeper, and make sure she doesn't go in the sea without me.' She leaned down close to the girl. 'No going into the water until I get back, do you hear me?'

'I want flowers,' was all she said.

'I'll get some more shells. You can put them on the roof, or make a path with them. That's better than flowers,' the boy said.

The mother left and the boy went to the edge of the water with his bucket. He began digging with a spade. The child looked up the beach, then started to walk towards the path. I got up and followed her.

When she reached the path where hundreds of feet had worn the ground to hard, stony earth, she looked at the edges where a little grass grew and where she probably hoped that she would find dandelions.

'Do you want some flowers for the house you're building?' I said.

She looked up at me, surprised. 'Yes.'

'Well, I've got some nice flowers in my garden, they are very pretty. If you come with me, you can have some. Do you want to?'

'Yes,' she said and she began to follow me.

I made sure that we walked near people; that she was beside me, or a little behind me. I did not touch her and it is unlikely that others, preoccupied with their own children, would have noticed that we were walking away from the beach together. 'I want flowers. I'm building a house. Flowers grow in gardens. The beach grows shells and stones. No flowers.' and so she chatted almost without stopping, as we made our way up the path away from the beach towards Pensqidden Lane. It took less than ten minutes.

We went through the back garden gate and there I encouraged her to pick as many of the flowers as she wanted. 'Mummy told me you wanted some flowers,' I said. She took a large blue hydrangea at the back of the garden and, from the flower bed under the window, two dahlias and a large gladioli. She looked at them and me delightedly as she held the brightly coloured flowers in her hand.

'Come in and have a drink after your long walk, you must be very thirsty.'

She hesitated before coming into the house, but she came and drank the orange juice I poured. I chatted to her throughout and took out some of Krystina's toys to amuse her. I still had some food in the house, cereal, milk, fruit, stale bread, a tin of beans, potatoes and some chocolate.

'I'll make you something to eat, now,' I said.

I knew there would be problems and I was prepared for them.

'I must go to the beach. Mummy gets the food.'

'And she wants you to have chips tonight, doesn't she?'

The child looked at me and I saw the uncertainty in her face.

'Yes, I know she does. She told me you wanted some flowers and some chips. She can't cook tonight and she wants me to look after you. She has to go away. That's why she told me to give you some chips, then you can watch television before bedtime.'

'Where is Mummy? Mummy didn't say goodbye. I want Jago.'

I heard the distress in her voice. I knew, too, how Krystina would have reacted if suddenly she had been taken away from me, or my mother, or Diane. I should have felt sorry for her, but I couldn't afford to. I needed the child. I needed to survive. I could not afford to feel pity for this one, at least she was alive.

★

I am reluctant to write about this. It is painful now for me to record these events and shame almost prevents me from doing so. I only know that, at the time, I was compelled by such terrible circumstances to continue with an unpremeditated plan, which seemed to present itself and was unfolding at that moment when the opportunity arose. I had never stolen anything in my life and I never intended to steal a child. When I did, it seemed to be the most natural thing to do. The theft would somehow replace what was lost, it might help to fill the gaping void in my heart.

So I told myself, so I chose to believe. We all choose what we believe and we censor our thoughts to make them acceptable to ourselves, to make that which is unbearable bearable. We choose our own narrative and we justify our own interpretation of that narrative. My own predicament was great and the future seemed to collapse before me. There was too much to lose and there could be no going back. The abduction was necessary. My life depended on it.

'I want Mummy! I want to go home! I want Mummy!' The tears began to flow.

I gently took her hands in mine. I spoke calmly . 'You've been living with Mummy for a long time. She's been looking after you, hasn't she?'

'And Jago and Daddy!'

'Yes, that's right. They've been looking after you, haven't they?'

'Yes.'

'Now, I'm here! I've been away for a long time. Now I've come back. Don't you remember me?

There was a small shake of the head.

'No? Perhaps you will, later on. But you will get to know me again."

'What's your name?'

'Don't you remember? My name is MummyClaire.'

'That's a funny name. When can I see my Mummy?'

'Not today. She wants you to get used to me, to MummyClaire. You can see her another day. Don't worry. You'll like staying with me. It's only for a short time. We can go out in the car tomorrow. That will be nice. Tonight we can watch television. Now, would you like some chips?'

She nodded hesitantly, doubtful, but unable to grasp the full implication of my words. I began to peel and cut the potatoes and then I fried them in some salad oil. She ate them in front of the small black and white television and this served to distract her for a while. I made her a hot drink of chocolate which she drank while still watching the television.

Soon after, I heard the sound of the helicopter circling over the bay.

I ran a warm bath for her, undid the small ponytail and washed her hair. She was comfortable in water, unlike

Krystina, and she did not cry when water went over her head. I gave her a yellow duck with which I used to entice Krystina in a bath of shallow water, but she took no interest in it. I chatted all the while, saying how tangled her hair was, how much sand there was in it, how it was impossible to brush, how we would have to cut a little bit off, it was the only way to get rid of the tangles.

I cut a little off, about two inches and showed her. 'See, it's not much, is it?'

She looked unconvinced but nodded in agreement just the same.

I got one of Krystina's nightdresses for her and she said, 'I wear jamjams in bed.'

'Oh, I got these specially for you! But never mind, we'll get you some pyjamas tomorrow.'

'Will Mummy come tomorrow?'

'Well, I don't know if Mummy can come here tomorrow, she knows we're going to go out in the car. Let's think about what we'll do tomorrow.'

I put her to bed, gave her a cuddly toy rabbit, read her a story. She paid little attention to the story, but held the rabbit close to her and eventually fell asleep. I watched her throughout the night. She slept with much tossing and turning. At one point I cut a little more off her hair, so it ended up quite short.

Early next morning I talked to her continually, while dressing her in Krystina's clothes which were at least one size too small for her. I told her she had grown since the last time I saw her. She ate some cereal, then we got in the car and I played Krystina's Disney tapes throughout the drive to

Plymouth. She kept touching her hair and eventually asked where her ponytail was. I said we had to cut some of it off because of tangles the night before, didn't she remember? But not to worry, it would grow again soon.

She fell asleep in the car for part of the journey and when we arrived I went straight to the large department stores. We went up and down the escalators, which she hadn't seen before; we went into toy departments and I bought whatever she wanted, although she only seemed to want a large beach ball and a small red car.

'I want a car for Jago,' she said.

'Well, I think Jago is going shopping today.'

She looked disappointed and I saw her eyes fill with tears.

'We can buy another car if you want to.'

Her face lit up and she chose another small car, a blue one.

She seemed to cheer up after that and so we went to eat in the cafeteria. She had fishcakes, peas and chips and managed to eat most of her food. I left most of mine for I was on edge throughout, conscious of not drawing attention to ourselves, yet trying to behave normally, afraid that anything she said would be heard by others.

We spent the afternoon going from one shop to another, looking for clothes. I bought her whatever she said she liked. At my suggestion, she tried on shorts, dungarees, sandals, a blue t shirt, a cap. She saw herself in a mirror then, but with the cap on she seemed not to notice her short hair. She looked like a boy. I guessed that she was a few months older than Krystina, maybe three years old; she was a little taller, more articulate, with a wider vocabulary.

We walked a lot that day and city life is tiring, so when we stopped for tea she was hungry and ate chocolate cake and ice cream and drank orange juice. I bought food to take back, anything she said she liked. We drove back to the songs of the 'Jungle Book' and 'Mary Poppins' and I encouraged her to join in with the singing. Together we sang the same songs over and over again. Ten minutes before we arrived back, close to nine o'clock, she fell asleep in the car and I carried her straight up to bed, taking off only her sandals and cap. She was tired out.

It was about half an hour later that I heard a knock on the door. I looked through the window first, to see who it was. It was Mr. Evans, owner of the house.

'Sorry to bother you, but I have to search the premises.'

'Search the premises?'

'Yes, it's the missing child.'

My heart began to beat wildly. 'Missing child? What missing child?'

'Haven't you heard? Child went missing yesterday late afternoon. They think she drowned, tide was on its way out. But it don't look like it. 'Least it's not certain. Too many people in the water, they think she wandered off, went off looking for flowers. Besides, they would've found a body by now.' He took off his cap as he came in the house. 'Now, say you drown at Land's End, then you're not likely to find the body again, but in these parts here, it's likely the next tide will bring it in.'

'So, why are you looking here?'

He noticed the tremor in my voice and he looked at me carefully.

'No need for you to worry, my luvver, just make sure you keep the doors and windows closed. They're asking everyone around here to check the premises. Children wander off, they get shut in sheds, cellars, well, some people leave doors open, you never know where little ones get sometimes. 'Least, that's how the thinking goes.'

'So, you want to check the garden, the garage?'

'I'll do that dreckly. First, the house. I got three of these houses here, all let. There's two men are sharing the one upalong, three doors from here, and, well, you know what I mean by that.'

I must have looked blank.

'Well, you never know, it takes all sorts. I went through their house, every room, very careful, didn't miss an inch, and I have to treat everyone the same, you know what I mean? Well, I'm the owner, so, sort of responsible like. So, I'll just be having a look round.'

I could do no other than stand back and watch as he looked around the living room, the kitchen and in the small cupboard which served as a larder. Then he started to go upstairs.

'My daughter is in bed, she's sleeping.'

'Oh, don't you worry, I won't wake her.'

I followed him up the stairs in a state of nervous apprehension. He went into the first bedroom, glanced around and went to the built-in cupboard. He opened the door and, although there was still a lot of light in the room, he shone his torch over my clothes hanging up, then over the holdall at the bottom. He came out and went in the smaller bedroom. The curtains were drawn so he shone the torch around the room. It rested for a few seconds on the child's head, on her short dark hair, on the white pillow.

'Fast asleep,' he whispered.

As I let him out of the house he said, 'I'll have a look at the garden and the garage now.'

I went with him as he walked around the garden, looking over shrubs and the blue hydrangeas at the back.

'The garden needs a bit of tidying up, Mr. Evans,' I said.

He looked around. 'Yes, I s'pose you're right. I'll try to come round, in the next day or two, before the new tenants come.'

'I can do that, Mr. Evans, if you like. In fact, I thought of doing it anyway. Krystina's got a bit over tired, so we're staying in tomorrow and there's nothing I like better than pottering around the garden. I find it very relaxing. There's not a lot to do anyway.'

'Well, if you really want to, that's awright by me. You've got all the stuff in that garage. I see you got the car in. It's a bit of a squeeze coming in from the lane.'

'Oh, it's fine, Mr. Evans, it's better than leaving it unprotected in the street. I'll tidy up the garden tomorrow and return the keys early on Saturday. We have a long way to go.'

'Well, I'll see you Saturday morning, then. You enjoy the rest of your holiday.'

With that he left and I went back and poured a glass of wine. I turned on the television and watched the news. There I saw the Trewins making a tearful plea for people to check their gardens, their homes, and if anyone had seen her, or thought they had seen her, knew where she was, please tell the police, 'Please, please, bring Merryn back to us.'

I turned off the television. At least I knew the name of the child in the upstairs bedroom. It was a pity the name was so unlike Krystina.

★

It was nearly midnight when I went into the garden and got a shovel from the garage. There was no light in the upstairs bedroom next door, which overlooked most of the garden but probably not the side of the house. Still I had to be watchful.

I avoided the area attached to the next house because the kitchen was on that side and I knew I had to avoid drains and pipes underground. I dug into the soil under the living room window, carefully lifting spadefuls with the flowers and their roots still attached and placing each one on the side of the garden by the wall. Then I dug, dug like a convict sentenced to hard labour. I thought of nothing but completing this task, as I dug with grim single-mindedness, piling the earth up to one side as if my life depended on it. It took me three hours to dig a grave, which was over four feet deep and nearly four feet long.

I wrapped a blanket around the holdall, for warmth, I told myself, and placed it down on the hard, cold earth. I sat a long time looking down at the small and lonely coffin, in a grave which was horribly large. Only when the sky was getting lighter did I summon up the will to shovel the earth on top and once the bag, covered with a pink blanket, had disappeared from sight, I hurriedly, in frantic, sweeping movements, filled the grave with earth. There was some excess earth and this I took to the back of the garden and spread it around the tree. I replanted the flowers, keeping each spadeful in the order in which I had removed them.

It was gone four when I went in, poured a half tumbler of whisky and fell asleep in the chair.

I woke three hours later, to the sound of a voice next to me.

'See Mark today? Go to Trickle?'

I turned to answer. A pallid early morning light oozed sickeningly through dull curtains across sparse, drab furniture. The room was drained of life. Then I heard the child upstairs crying.

She was wet and crying fretfully. Tired and slightly groggy, I told her it didn't matter, we would play with her new ball and car in the garden, she could help me tidy it up, watch me cut the grass, dig up weeds. I put her in the bath, changed the bed, washed the sheets. I made breakfast, putting everything I had bought the day before on the table, told her to choose what she wanted. She chose cornflakes and hot chocolate and chocolate cake and then she was sick. I changed her clothes, washed her again and told her to sit still while I read stories. It was going to be a difficult day.

She asked questions constantly, the same ones over and over again. Where is Mummy? Where is Daddy? Where is Jago? When can we see Mummy? When will Daddy come here? Can I play with Jago today? Can I give him his car?

'Not now,' I would reply. 'You are living with MummyClaire now. Grandma used to look after you. Now I'm looking after you.'

'I don't live with Granny! I don't live with you. I live with Mummy and Daddy and Jago! I want to go home! Where is Mummy?'

'I told you, Mummy wants me to look after you now, just for a while. Granny is sick and Mummy has to look after her. When Granny is better, you can go back home.'

'Where is Daddy?'

'Daddy is working.'

'I want Jago. I want to play with Jago. We can play with the cars.'

'Not today. Jago is helping Mummy because he is older. You can play with your cuddly rabbit. You can play with your new toys. Look at the pictures in the book. You can draw pictures. Look at these crayons, aren't they pretty colours? Draw a picture for MummyClaire.'

And so it went on throughout the morning. My whole body ached. I was exhausted and feverish. I realized how difficult the next few days would be, how close I could come to being discovered.

That was the day, the morning after I had buried Krystina, that I fully realized the enormity of what I had undertaken and the vilification I would face if I failed. I had to win and I knew then that I would have to be constantly vigilant as the days merged into weeks and months and even years. It will get easier, I told myself, given time, it will get easier.

I cut the grass with the ancient grass cutter stored in the garage. I let the child help me to push it and this kept her occupied for a while. I pulled up the weeds, tidied all the flowerbeds, turned the earth over. I filled a watering can and we sprinkled water on the flowerbeds. She seemed to enjoy this so we repeated the process until she tired of it. The garden looked spring-cleaned. There was nothing to arouse suspicion. It was gone two in the afternoon when I finished and we had tomato soup with bread for lunch. She ate this and seemed more settled and I read more stories.

Later in the afternoon I brought a box of toys into the

garden, but she took only a desultory interest and became restless, then agitated and she started asking me again. 'When can I go home? I want to go home.' When I said, 'Not yet, you're staying with me now for a few days, we'll have a nice time,' she didn't answer.

It was about a minute later when she started screaming, 'I don't want to stay with you! You are not my mummy!'

As I ran to get her, to silence her, for there were people in the next garden, she ran away from me, trying to reach the gate, then she hid behind the tree all the time screaming in rage, 'I want to go home! You are not my mummy!'

I caught her up roughly, clamped my hand over her mouth and carried her, a fighting, kicking, screaming, convulsive fiend, into the house. I went into the kitchen, opened a drawer which contained various odd items and where I had seen some sellotape. This I grabbed and gripping her head into the crook of my arm I clumsily, awkwardly, tore off short strips, sticking four or five layers, roughly, forcefully, over her mouth and across her cheeks. I forced her arms into the arms of my cotton jacket, tying the long ends behind her back, like a straightjacket. I carried her to the bathroom, and closed the windows and door.

The house seemed very quiet and I breathed deeply, trying to calm myself down, before hurrying into the garden and looking over the hedge at the new neighbours next door, still curiously looking at the house. I apologised for the screaming. 'I'm sorry. It's tantrum stage, I'm afraid.'

'She did sound very upset,' said the woman in a flowered dress, her own docile toddler twins, playing nearby. Was she suspicious?

'She's missing her grandmother,' I said. 'I was in hospital for quite a long time and my mother looked after her. Most of the time she's fine with me but when she can't get her own way, she wants her grandma.'

'Oh, I understand. It must be difficult for you and you can't let them rule you or they'll take over. Don't worry, you need to be firm. She'll soon learn.' Flowered dress seemed to be satisfied.

This, and Mr. Evan's visit the previous evening, were the times I came closest to being discovered. They left me severely shaken and the fear I felt then strengthened my resolve to be firm with her. I had to be ruthless, I could not allow her to betray me. She must do as she was told.

Two hours passed and two more whiskies and a cup of tea, before I felt sufficiently in control to release her from her prison. She was subdued, sobbing quietly, all violence gone. I took off the jacket and tape, spoke gently to her, washed her, put on the new pyjamas, and gave her beans on toast. I took her to my bed and put a teaspoon of whisky in her mug of warm milk and honey. I had another glass of whisky myself and by the time I had finished reading the first story she was asleep and, with occasional whimpering, kicking and turning, she slept throughout the night.

*

The next day the local paper was filled with news about the missing child. There were pictures of Merryn on the front page; police were appealing for witnesses, anyone who had seen something suspicious; beaches and coves were still being searched. We left very early in the car and drove as far away as possible. Devon beaches, also crowded, felt safer and I took her into the sea with me. She loved the water and for a time seemed to enjoy being there, but for the most part she was quiet and unresponsive.

Returning late and tired in the evening almost ensured a peaceful night. She ate little and went to bed without complaint.

Our time in Cornwall was coming to an end and we spent the penultimate day in Newquay. I phoned my mother from a phone box, the child cramped in behind me, eating sweets.

I told my mother I had decided to go to France before coming home. 'It makes sense to go straight there rather than going all the way home, only to set off for the port a day or two later, when it's much closer to us here.'

'Don't you think Krystina has had enough excitement for a while? Don't overdo it. Let me speak to her.'

'Say hello to Grandma, Krystina,' I said quietly into the phone and then added, 'Come on, it's Grandma, now don't be shy.' I waited a few seconds before, raising my voice, I said, 'Oh, she's looking at the telephone as if she's never seen one before. She can hear your voice …'

So I prattled on, with my back to the child who was gazing out of the window, until my mother said, 'Oh, don't worry, don't make her speak on the phone if she doesn't want to. Children get like that. She'll talk enough when she gets back home.'

My mother had no idea of the effort and pain this conversation caused me and I felt exhausted after the phone call. I was torn between fear and relief. I had no choice but to dissemble, to practise an outrageous level of deceit on those closest and dearest to me, a deception I would have to maintain for the rest of my life. At that moment, I saw myself clearly. I knew what I was, knew what I was capable of. I came close to being sick, there in the phone box, with the child beside me drearily eating sweets. I was a liar, a deceiver, a child snatcher. Self-contempt swept through me, poisonous in its septicity. No one could have hated me at that moment more than I hated myself.

17

Those last days in Cornwall, ominous with bright sunshine, crowded beaches and crowded towns, the dubious attractions typical of a robust tourist industry and an endless trail of car journeys, finally came to an end. I drove away in tears, tormented by recurring images of Krystina and Mark, the memory of one forever linked with the other. Only as we crossed the Tamar was I able to focus a little on our escape and I breathed a little easier.

I didn't like the child. She had none of Krystina's natural sweetness, none of the little outbursts of giggles, none of the affection, those moments when she would come and sit on my lap, snuggle up to me as I read a story.

The child was morose, sullen, uncooperative. She said nothing while I drove to Southampton, telling her about the wonderful holiday we would have in France.

'Can Jago come, too?' she asked.

'Not this time, maybe next time.'

'Will Mummy be there?'

'Not today. She's looking after Granny. She wants you to be a good girl and go on a nice holiday with MummyClaire.'

As soon as she saw the boats, she kicked and screamed in

the car seat. 'I don't want to go on the boat! I don't want to go with you! You are not my mummy!'

We were in the long queue of cars waiting to embark. I had to silence her. She had to understand there were boundaries she could not cross.

I held her by the arms and said firmly, too firmly, 'You must not say that! Never again! Do you understand? Do you want me to tie you up and leave you in the back of the car on your own? Do you? Do you? DO YOU?" I stared into her eyes and knew that she was afraid of me. She became quiet and eventually tearfully muttered, 'No.'

We could not draw attention to ourselves. I told myself that many a parent had done far worse and under these circumstances, such treatment could not be avoided, a little unkindness was inevitable. It was necessary to avoid detection. I needed her cooperation, whether she gave it freely or not, and I was determined to get it. It was necessary.

On the boat, she just looked out of the window in the passenger lounge to the sea, every so often saying, 'I want to go home,' in a low, plaintive voice.

'Later,' I would say, 'we have a nice home in France. You went there once when you were a little baby. Do you remember that?'

She shook her head and said, 'I want to go back to Mummy.'

'You mustn't say that! You are going home now, with MummyClaire.'

Fearing that other passengers sitting near would overhear us, I took her for a walk on the deck and tried to distract her by talking about boats and what we would see in France. It was impossible to divert her from whatever she was thinking, she showed little interest and walked beside me like an automaton as I kept my hand on her shoulder, keeping her close to me at all times. Thinking constantly of Krystina while paying attention to this child and always watching and listening was extremely tiring. I was exhausted. I longed for sleep.

Having embarked safely, without suspicion or questions from anyone, I thought I would begin to feel some relief, a sense of liberation, however temporary. Instead, I was anxious, afraid, my nerves were in shreds, I jumped at any unexpected sound. I had reached the limit of my strength and endurance. I could not go on. Hope sank as depression engulfed me.

As the boat made its way across the channel and I saw England slipping further and further away, grief and remorse flooded through me. I had lost so much: a precious, delightful child, the man I loved, the family and friends whom I would not see for years, perhaps never again. Even as I cut myself off from the past, the memory would continue to gnaw its way into every moment of my waking life. The future looked bleak and menacing.

Such was the desolation which held my whole being in thrall, that I forgot about the child standing, miserable and silent, beside me. An anguished loneliness overwhelmed me and bitter tears fell copiously as I leaned over the railings of the boat and looked into the deep water just a few meters below. I longed to sink into that dark, heaving swell, to be taken down deep onto the seabed and to stay there forever more. The sea became my friend, it invited me in and offered deliverance and a solution. I raised one foot purposefully on to the railing, eager for the comfort of cold oblivion.

It was the child's sudden grip on my hand, a grip no doubt occasioned by fear and incomprehension, that made me turn my gaze from the turbulent water beneath and look at her pale, anxious face. She was a forlorn little girl, apprehensive, bewildered, alone in a sea of strangers. What could she understand? What would she do now? What would happen to her? At that moment I was all she had.

Minutes may have passed while I felt the sea like a magnet pulling me towards it and her hand holding on to mine, claiming it as something owed to her.

I do not remember the actual moment when I made the decision, but I found myself walking along the deck, hastily drying tears, with the child trudging along beside me, her face pale, expressionless.

I knew I had to remain calm, knew I must be gentle with her and patient. I had a duty of care which I had failed disastrously with my own child, but I would succeed with this one. That much I owed her. She was my lifeline, my only way of escaping cataclysmic ruin.

As the coast of France came in view I vowed to make it up to her. I would devote my life to her. I would atone. She would be my redemption.

18

It was late afternoon when I booked in at a small hotel for the night and soon after went to the restaurant. I spoke to the waiter in French, made some remarks about French and English to the child and said casually, 'Now, eat your food, Krystina, that's a good girl.'

It was the first time I had used a name when speaking to her. I had difficulty doing so; the name did not belong to her. It was painful for me to use my child's name and my voice broke as I said it; but I had no choice, it was necessary. She ate slowly, almost thoughtfully.

'The food is very nice. Did you like it, Krystina?' I asked casually.

'My name is Merryn.'

'But in French that name is Krystina. Everyone here calls you Krystina. It's a nice name, isn't it?'

'My name is Merryn! Merryn! Merryn!" she shouted, defiance written on her face.

'Of course,' I said soothingly, 'so it is. But we all have more than one name don't we? Here, they call you Krystina, it's just while we're in France.'

I tried not to call her Krystina too often, although, once

we were in the chateau, it was impossible to avoid doing so completely. She did not take easily to the name and did not always respond when spoken to. She regarded my uncle and aunt with suspicion, but my warnings had taught her to be careful. She remembered what I was capable of and was unduly quiet with them at first and glanced at me whenever they spoke to her, as if waiting for my approval; but after a month or so, she began to answer them with a few words.

She played with the toy cars, sometimes talking as she did so. 'This is for you, Jago. The blue one is for you. I chose it for you. My car is red.' When Uncle Martin overheard her one day, I merely shrugged, smiled, and said, 'An imaginary friend; apparently, he drives the blue car.'

I became weary of the almost constant requests to go home and, once, when she said yet again, 'I want to go home' I knelt down in front of her, grabbed her arms and looked at her sternly, 'Do not say that again! This is your home! Understand?' She was wary of me and when she said it again, soon after, I repeated the action. Over the next hour, she did not speak at all and I began to praise her, 'You are a very good girl, Krystina. You do what MummyClaire tells you. Good girl.'

When we went out she would gaze at people, scrutinizing the faces of every woman, man and young boy. Once, in the vineyard she suddenly ran from me, up to two of the workers, and asked them, 'Can you find my mummy?' Their lack of English made the question harmless, but when I caught her, I gripped her wrist, and told her I would shut her in her room when we returned to the chateau.

Walking back, I knew she was frightened and soon she tried to placate me by saying she liked the house and the grapes and she actually, for the first time, called me MummyClaire. I did take her to our room when we got back, but stayed with her and when she promised to be good I praised her and read a story to her. She seemed to like being read to, perhaps, for her as well as for me, it offered a brief escape from reality.

I made sure she ate good food, sweets and chocolate had all but disappeared, and she responded well, eating without complaint. I rewarded her with praise. Each night I managed to praise her for something while she drank the warm milk and honey which helped her to sleep and only very occasionally, in those early days, did I need to add a teaspoon of whisky at the end of a difficult day.

Slowly, she realized, like a Pavlov dog, that compliance brought its own rewards. She was quiet and pensive by day, but before going to sleep she would often ask when we would see Jago; and on those nights she would fall asleep holding the toy car she chose for him.

As soon as we arrived in Australia and she heard English again she thought we were going home. 'Will I see my other Mummy again now?'

My answer was always the same. 'Not today. Don't you remember? Mummy wants you to go on holiday with MummyClaire. She wants you to have a nice time.'

Looking after the child, dragging her with me from one scenic view to another, one winery after another, kept me going. All the places we visited were names on a map, evidence of activity, evidence of moving on, of moving away. I did not feel safe. I could not stay in one place for long. I was always on the move, hunted by fear, haunted by memory.

The questions, the confusion and the unhappiness of the child weighed on my conscience. There were times when she sat looking ahead, saying nothing, seemingly unaware of anything around her. There were tears which came suddenly, sometimes during the day, most often at night. I understood what she was going through and I tried to comfort her, but I could not restore what she had lost, anymore than I could restore what I had lost. She took the small blue car to bed with her, clutching the hard metal to her as some children might clutch a favourite doll.

I felt better when she responded to the hectic schedule of different tourist attractions, which went some way to distract her, and when she slowly began to show some interest and even to laugh. Our travels in Australia, so different from the life we had been living before, helped to entertain and distract her, they provided her with new experiences, new memories shared together. I talked to her, I read to her every day, stories for children, about children. I tried to establish routines to give her the security she needed.

Those months were spent painfully protecting, nurturing, and yoking another child to me. I talked about Martin and Carla, the chateau, the vineyard, reminding her of food we had eaten there, where we had walked. Later, I talked to her about my mother, Diane, the shop and our life in Sussex.

Gradually, the memory of her own family began to fade, she mentioned them less often. She began to mix some of her memories with mine. Slowly, carefully, I familiarised her with a family which would become her own. I aimed to eliminate all memory of Cornwall.

Looking after her was both a burden and a consolation.

She was not Krystina and part of me had resented her for it, yet she reminded me of her so much that I grew fond of her. I cared for her as well as I could because we needed each other.

It was a lonely, gruelling time for me. I was thin and anxious, racked by memories and dreams. The death of a child ravishes every waking moment; and at the end of each long, bleak day I felt that I would die from grief. This sorrow had to be hidden, it could never be revealed, none could comfort, help or console. Few, knowing my story, would want to do so.

★

It was in Christchurch that I realized, suddenly and unexpectedly, how much I had achieved and how completely she had accepted me. By then, she had stopped asking to go home; home really became wherever we were living at the time. She had consigned the blue and red cars to the toy box and, much later, would give them to James, her brother. When she used my name, it was usually Claire, and, sometimes, Mummy. By then she remembered no mother other than myself. It had taken nearly three years.

It was at this time, too, that my own tormented feelings became less acutely painful; and I only learned to accept the loss of my child when the living child had become part of me. She was mine, the name was now hers; she had, in my mind and to all intents and purposes, become Krystina.

Now, this is how she sees herself. It is *who* she is. She *believes* what I have told her of her past; she *knows* what she has learnt and experienced, thought and done since. This is an essential part of her character, her personality, her sense of self. It cannot be undone.

Identity is not about a name, a legal nicety, or physical appearance. We grow and age, physically and mentally. Our bodies do not remain the same, neither do our minds; and few would recognize us after a thirty year absence. Over such a time, we may not even recognize ourselves as we once were. That self, which we think we know, is constantly modified as we live through a flux of change, choosing the memories that feed our sense of worth, censoring those which challenge the image we have of ourselves. In that sense we create our own identity.

Krystina knows who she is. She has moved far away from the Trewins, she has no connection with them, they are different people and she is no longer the child they knew.

We had both suffered and recovered together all those years ago; we had become whole again and together we started a new life. A close bond, the closest bond of all, developed between us, that bond between mother and child, and it has stood the test of time.

*

This is the story which I never wanted to reveal and no good can come now from this confession. It will not help Krystina. As Krystina Bentley she has had a good life, with devoted parents who have cherished and loved her and a brother who adores her. She is happy, fulfilled, successful. Isn't that all we want for our children? I have not harmed her. Bad things happen to all of us. We get over them and life moves on. The past is over; we live only in the present and I refuse to be defined by what I did then, thirty years ago.

I will end here. It is late morning and it cannot be long now. My papers are on the table beside me: financial documents, the deeds to my property, my will. My story, if needed, will be placed with them, perhaps within the hour.

19

Yet, as I sit here, waiting, I know I am deluding myself and doubt eats into me as the minutes tick away.

Time may allay our fears, offer mitigation, even comfort and console, but we still have to live with the consequences of those actions which shape us and make us what we are. It does not absolve us of culpability, or take away responsibility.

Good results may come from a bad action, but they do not make the action good. It is the burglar, no matter how desperate the motivation, who is guilty, not the householder who fails to lock the door. I hear Cynthia Trewin's words, *But I am to blame, I left them alone.* The guilt falls on me, not on the mother who goes to a shop, or a brother who digs in the sand.

It is all in the past now and time cannot be relived. Krystina is my child, more mine than hers, by thirty years. I can see her now, her attention divided between us, sympathy extended to both, for different reasons far beyond her understanding. I hear the words they spoke, see the way they looked, the easy, natural communication between them, some inherent attraction.

I look and I listen in an armchair from which I am too weak and too frightened to move. I see what might have been and I feel for them, feel for them both. Yes, I feel for Cynthia Trewin for my tragedy is also hers. I am aware of what I have done.

Yesterday, while I was alone, she was with them all – mother, father, brother, sister. What did they talk about in all those hours? What memories were revived? What observations made? What effect did the reclusive Jago have? What more does Cynthia Trewin now know? *It's easy to imagine a resemblance. The mind plays tricks, suddenly, when you least expect it.*

They would look at the painting. A beach scene: sand, sea, sky, children playing, swimming, paddling, sandcastles, buckets, spades. *I find it a little disturbing.* What was it that so arrested her attention? Something resonated, something that required further attention, something to be shared. *It's very interesting.* She wanted Jago to see it.

He was there, the brother who lives alone, works alone and rescues people from the sea. An attractive man. I saw the resemblance – perhaps I only imagined it – as I gazed with reluctant fascination at the photograph his mother had put in my hands. *They were close …* I see him now, at the water's edge, digging for shells, a boy who looked away. *He was never quite the same after Merryn disappeared.*

Am I also responsible for this?

What would Krystina see, feel, understand? *We were there thirty years ago, isn't that a strange coincidence?* It was only the tree, the tree in the garden, the single residual memory, which resurfaced in her mind. Nothing more.

One memory. It was enough to set her on a path of discovery and, with unfortunate timing, all else followed naturally, precipitously.

My reaction, I see it clearly now, was aggressive, unnatural. With devious, clumsy responses I had aroused her suspicions. *You're hiding something from me.*

She knew me too well. I was tense, on edge, caught in a time trap, pursued by a memory , constantly wanting to run, run far away as I had done before. *You haven't been yourself. You sound like a stranger* ... her words stung me.

Yet, after the anger, there had been a conciliatory offer. *There's something you're not telling me. Wouldn't it help if you told me?*

Just tell me, and I could have told her. For a moment, the briefest of moments, I imagine relief flooding through me, washing away thirty years of concealment.

But I see the stunned, incredulous look on her face, the shock, the confusion, the sudden loss of trust, the awareness of betrayal. I see how ... No, I could not think of it, could not do it, not then, not ever.

I have deceived her, taken away that which was rightfully hers.

I cannot put right the wrong I have done. It is too late. Love alone is not enough to atone for my deception, neither does it redeem me.

What good would revelation of past, forgotten events do now? Her identity, her name, her sense of self, cannot be changed, they are who she is.

It would do more harm than good to contrast her past and all that she remembers of it, with what might have been, what should have been.

For thirty years I have been her mother. This is her past, as it is mine, it cannot be changed. It is too late to return what was lost, too late for expiation. Dwelling on what should have been and what could have been is mere speculation.

★

Twenty-four hours have passed since I left that ill-fated land and my mind wanders restlessly, tormented by questions which I cannot answer. I do not know and I have no way of knowing what happened yesterday. *It's not knowing, that's the worst part.*

I mourn for the child I lost and I mourn for the one I fear I am about to lose. There is nothing I can do and it is breaking me.

I can only wait. Past and present now race towards each other and I foresee the collision which may follow. It is my hour of reckoning and I am afraid.

I must not despair, not yet. It may have been nothing more than an ordinary day out, a few hours spent sympathetically with a family who had lost a child thirty years ago. Nothing more. She may return willingly to me, curiosity satisfied, pleased to be home. A happy ending.

She belongs here. I have loved her. I love her still. I will not let imagination run away with me.

I feel a stream of confidence flowing into me, a growing optimism. I begin to hope for Krystina's safe return to me, her mother.

Merryn Trewin died a long time ago. She must return as Krystina Bentley It is in her interest to do so, as it is in mine. I cannot lose her twice.

Yet even as I think these words, even as hope rises within me, Cynthia Trewin, patient and long-suffering, drifts through my mind like a passing ghost.

20

The phone rings at ten minutes past twelve and I pick it up instantly.

'Hello?'

'I'm just leaving now. I'll be back later this afternoon.'

She speaks calmly, efficiently.

'Krystina...'

But she cuts in abruptly before I can continue. 'It's time we went to the police to make a statement.'

'Did you go this morning?'

'No, I haven't spoken to them yet. I thought it would be better if I went with you. They'll need our DNA.'

'DNA?'

'Yes, I'm sure you understand.'

'Krystina...'

'We can go together, but we need to talk first.'

And she puts the phone down.